THE SCIENTIFIC LIFE OF AZALEAH LANE

BY NIKKI SHANNON SMITH

ILLUSTRATED BY GLORIA FELIX

PICTURE WINDOW BOOKS
a capstone imprint

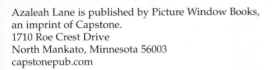

Azaleah Lane is published by Picture Window Books,
an imprint of Capstone.
1710 Roe Crest Drive
North Mankato, Minnesota 56003
capstonepub.com

Library of Congress Cataloging-in-Publication Data
Names: Smith, Nikki Shannon, 1971- author. | Félix, Gloria, illustrator. |
Smith, Nikki Shannon, 1971- Azaleah Lane.
Title: The scientific life of Azaleah Lane / by Nikki Shannon Smith ;
illustrated by Gloria Felix.
Description: North Mankato, Minnesota : Picture Window Books, an
imprint of Capstone, [2021] | Series: Azaleah Lane | Audience: Ages
5–7. | Audience: Grades K–1. | Summary: Third-grader Azaleah Lane
has been chosen STEM lab monitor for the week, but on her first day,
Harry, the lab guinea pig, gets out of his cage and escapes. Azaleah has
to figure out a strategy to locate where in the room he is hiding and catch
him. But she also has another problem—how to get Terrance to listen and
work with the group on their Rube Goldberg machine project.
Identifiers: LCCN 2021002532 (print) | LCCN 2021002533 (ebook) |
ISBN 9781515844679 (hardcover) | ISBN 9781515844716 (ebook pdf)
Subjects: LCSH: African American girls—Juvenile fiction. | Middle-born
children—Juvenile fiction. | Guinea pigs—Behavior—Juvenile fiction. |
Science projects—Juvenile fiction. | Cooperativeness—Juvenile fiction. |
Washington (D.C.)—Juvenile fiction. | CYAC: Science projects—Fiction. |
Gduinea pigs—Fiction. | Animals—Habits and behavior—Fiction. |
Cooperativeness—Fiction. | Schools—Fiction. | African Americans—
Fiction. | Washington (D.C.)—Fiction.
Classification: LCC PZ7.S6566 Sc 2021 (print) | LCC PZ7.S6566 (ebook) |
DDC 813.6 [Fic]—dc23
LC record available at https://lccn.loc.gov/2021002532
LC ebook record available at https://lccn.loc.gov/2021002533

Image Credits: Shutterstock: Beskova Ekaterina, design element
throughout

Designer: Kay Fraser

TABLE OF CONTENTS

HEY, THERE! I'M AZALEAH!

I'm eight years old and in the third grade. My life is *amazing*. I live in Washington, D.C., with my family: Mama, Daddy, Nia, and Tiana. Washington, D.C., is our nation's capital and the *coolest* place to grow up.

Mama has her very own restaurant here called Avec Amour. That means "with love" in French. She named it that because she adds love to everything she does.

My daddy is a lawyer. He sues bad guys for a living. The bad guys are big businesses that do things that hurt other people. But my daddy makes them pay. He makes sure they're held responsible.

Tiana is my baby sister. She's four years old and pretty cute—most of the time. I like her a lot, even though she comes in my room too much. I also have an older sister named Nia. She's in middle school and is always in her room. *Always.*

Mama's sister—my Auntie Sam—takes care of us when Mama and Daddy are busy. I love Auntie Sam. She's never too tired to play, and she likes to do art. She also likes adventures—my favorite!

Aside from my family, there are three main things you should know about me.

1. I'm curious . . . *not* nosy. (Despite what Nia says.)

2. I'm good at solving mysteries—very good.

3. I live in the White House!

OK . . . not the *real* White House. (The president of the United States lives there.) But my house is big and white, plus it has a great big living room and a nice backyard. It's just as good as the real White House, if you ask me!

IT'S HARD TO BELIEVE THIS AMAZING LIFE ALL BELONGS TO ME, AZALEAH LANE!

CHAPTER 1

BAD MOOD MONDAY

I hopped out of bed Monday morning like a kangaroo. I had been waiting all weekend for today!

Monday was special announcements day at school. And today's announcements were *extra* special. Our principal, Ms. Li, was picking a third grader to be the STEM lab monitor for the week. Fifth graders had gotten the first turns. Then Ms. Li had picked fourth graders. The third graders had been waiting for a very long time. And guess who was a third grader? Me!

Please let Ms. Li pick me, I thought.

I washed up, got dressed, brushed my edges, and ran to the kitchen. My parents were already there. Mama had on her robe. She was staring out of the window with a cup of coffee in her hand. Daddy was at the table. He was wearing his robe too. His eyes were droopy like he was about to fall asleep.

"Good morning!" I said.

I sat down with Daddy. He smiled at me, but his lips were still asleep, so it was a very tiny smile.

Mama put homemade blueberry muffins, cantaloupe, and orange juice on the table. "Hi, Azaleah," she said.

"Guess what?" I asked.

Mama took a sip of coffee. Daddy stared at his muffin. They didn't say anything.

Since my parents didn't guess, I kept talking. "Today, Ms. Li is picking a third

grader to be the STEM lab monitor for the whole week. On Friday we all wrote our names on a ticket and put them in Ms. Li's glitter box. Today, she's shaking the box, closing her eyes, and picking out a name."

I crossed all of my fingers and hooked my thumbs together for good luck. I held them up and showed my hands to Daddy.

He said, "Mmm hmmm."

I frowned. Something wasn't right. Daddy and I were always the earliest early birds. But today he didn't have any energy at all.

"The STEM lab monitor is very important," I explained. "They take care of the STEM lab. They feed the animals and clean the cages and keep the lab clean. Sometimes they get to help Mr. Aguilar, the STEM lab teacher, set up activities."

My parents still didn't answer me. Mama sat down and stared at her coffee.

Daddy took a bite of his muffin. It reminded me of the time the batteries in my robot died. It got slower and slower, and then it stopped. My parents looked like they needed new batteries.

"What's wrong?" I asked.

"I'm just tired. I had a long night," said Mama. "I fed a hundred people last night."

I knew Mama had hosted a private party at her restaurant, Avec Amour. It was for the National Museum of African American History and Culture. But I didn't know it was that big. A hundred people was a lot!

"Wow, Mama," I said. "Avec Amour is really famous, huh?"

She nodded. Poor Mama was too tired to be excited. Owning the best restaurant in Washington, D.C., and being the best chef ever was hard work.

"You need a vacation, Mama," I said.

She smiled. "I'm on a mini-vacation now," she said. "I'm not working nights this week."

"Daddy, are *you* okay?" I asked.

"I stayed up too late," he said. "I was reading a good book. Then your sister—"

Before Daddy could finish, my little sister, Tiana, came into the kitchen. Her frown looked like one of those fish with a turned-down mouth. She was holding her favorite stuffie, Greenie, and her hair was sticking up all over her head. She tried to climb into Daddy's lap, but he wouldn't let her.

"Sit in a chair and eat your breakfast, okay?" he said.

Tiana whined and sat in a chair. But instead of eating, she started crying.

"Why are you crying?" I asked.

Tiana looked at me and let out a long cry.

"She had a bad dream in the middle of the night," said Daddy. "I had to lie in her bed with her until she fell asleep again. It took a few hours. She's tired."

No wonder Daddy looked like a zombie.

"Anyway," I said. I talked very loudly so they could hear me over Tiana's whining. "I hope I get to be the STEM lab monitor. There's a guinea pig named Harry, and he's so cute and fluffy. I would get to hold him and feed him!"

Tiana let out another big cry.

"Tiana, that's enough," said Mama.

I could tell Mama meant business. Tiana must have known it too because she closed her mouth and hugged Greenie.

Just then, our big sister, Nia, came in. Usually, Nia was very fancy. She always had on a cute outfit. But not today. Today, Nia had on jeans and an old T-shirt that said *The World Is My Stage*. She hadn't picked out her Afro, so it was flat on one side.

Nia was always trying different hairstyles. Lately she had been wearing it in an Afro because she was going to be Annie in her next school musical. Nia was always in a musical. Daddy called her a triple threat. She could sing and act and dance. She would probably be famous one day. She was already famous at her middle school.

"Guess what, Nia?" I said. "Today, Ms. Li is choosing a new STEM lab monitor! It's going to be a third grader. It might be *me*!"

Nia frowned and covered her ears. "Why is everyone being so loud? It's too early for this much noise."

My big sister was very dramatic. That's why she was such a good actor. But sometimes she was *too* dramatic, like right now. Right now she was dramatic *and* grouchy, and I knew why.

Nia had stayed up too late practicing for her musical. She had to memorize her lines and learn a bunch of songs. Last night, she had worked on her solo. It was a song about the sun coming out tomorrow. Her singing was so good, she sang me right to sleep.

I sighed. My exciting Monday was feeling more like bad-mood Monday. Everyone in my house was complaining—except for me.

Hopefully school would be better than our kitchen. Hopefully Ms. Li would announce my name, and I would be the best STEM lab monitor in the whole world.

I would impress Ms. Li. Then on Friday, when she announced weekly congratulations and recognitions, she would say my name again.

I could hear it now: "I would like to recognize Azaleah Lane for her fabulous work as the STEM lab monitor this week."

I couldn't wait to get to school. This might turn out to be the best day ever.

CHAPTER 2

SPECIAL ANNOUNCEMENTS

As soon as Daddy dropped me off at school, I spotted my best friend, Rose, on the playground. She was already standing in line, even though the bell hadn't rung yet.

"Hi, Rose!" I hollered. "Today, Ms. Li is picking a third grader for the STEM lab monitor job."

Rose grinned and did a little dance. "I know. It's finally our turn! I wonder who she'll pick."

The bell rang, and I jumped in line behind Rose. The rest of the class came running.

Somebody bumped someone else, and they started arguing. I could hear Terrance shouting about the STEM lab, even though he was all the way in the back of our line. Terrance was the most talkative person in my class.

Our teacher, Ms. Johnson, came out and stood in front of us. She waited for everyone to calm down, but my class was too excited.

Ms. Johnson let out a big sigh and started walking down the line. I knew she was giving reminders. That was when she had to tell you something she'd already told you before.

I peeked behind me and saw Ms. Johnson stop and whisper something to Terrance. He nodded and stood very still.

I made sure I was nice and quiet because I didn't want to be late. Ms. Li's announcements were first thing in the morning.

We finally got into our classroom. I sat at my table and looked at the board. The first thing on the schedule was announcements. Rose sat down across from me. I grinned at her and pointed to the board. She smiled back.

Our class was very noisy. Lots of kids were talking about the STEM lab monitor. Before Ms. Johnson could give out any more reminders, the intercom chime came on.

"Good morning, everyone," Ms. Li said over the speaker. "Happy Monday. It's time for our special announcements."

The whispering in my classroom stopped. Everyone stared at the speaker in the front of our classroom.

Please let it be me, I thought.

"Today, I'll be drawing the name of a third grader," Ms. Li continued. "That lucky person will be this week's STEM lab monitor!"

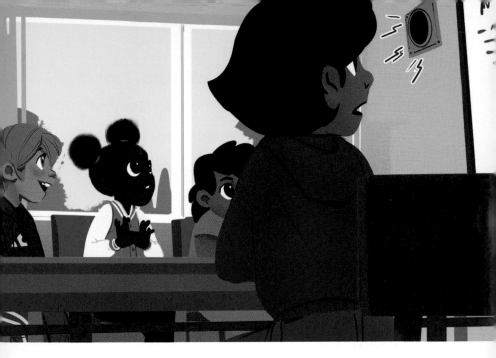

Rose and I looked at each other. Rose crossed her fingers. I crossed my fingers *and* thumbs.

"Can you hear that?" asked Ms. Li. The sound of paper rustling came through the speaker. "That's the sound of me shaking up the names in my glitter box. Now, I'm closing my eyes . . ."

My whole entire class held their breath.

" . . . and picking a name . . ."

There was silence while Ms. Li picked a ticket.

"This week's STEM lab monitor is . . . Azaleah Lane in Ms. Johnson's class!"

I grinned at Rose. She smiled with one side of her mouth. It looked like she was sad for herself and happy for me.

The other kids in my class sighed. I knew a lot of them wanted to be the STEM lab monitor. Some of them looked sad, so I worked very hard to be calm. I clapped a very soft clap and smiled at Ms. Johnson. She smiled back.

"Azaleah, please report to the lab at recess. I'll pick a new third grader next week," Ms. Li finished. "Have a good day, everyone!"

Now I had to wait all the way until morning recess to check in with Mr. Aguilar in the STEM lab. I couldn't wait to take Harry out of his cage and snuggle him. I would take good care of the lab. I was going to be an excellent monitor.

"I have a special announcement this morning too," said Ms. Johnson. "We are doing a special project this week. And it involves the STEM lab."

The whole class perked up. The sad kids looked less sad.

"What is it, Ms. Johnson?" asked Terrance. He didn't even raise his hand.

"You'll be working in groups to make something called a Rube Goldberg machine," she said. "And—"

"What's a Rube Goldberg machine?" Terrance interrupted. He still didn't raise his hand.

Ms. Johnson looked at him. I knew Terrance was about to get a reminder.

I was right. Ms. Johnson said, "Please raise your hand, Terrance."

Terrance raised his hand. "What's a Rube Goldberg machine?" he asked.

"A Rube Goldberg machine uses energy and a chain reaction to make something happen," explained Ms. Johnson. "Have you ever set up dominoes in a line, and then pushed over the first one?"

The class nodded.

"What happens when you do that?" she asked.

Terrance raised his hand and shouted at the same time. "They all fall over!"

"That's right. The first domino knocks over the second one, and then the second one knocks over the third one. It continues like that until they've all fallen down," said Ms. Johnson. "Each domino has energy. It can do work. When you knock one over, it gives its energy to the next domino. Then that one does work. Every time the energy makes something new happen, it's a chain reaction."

I never knew that energy was part of science. I always thought if you were moving around a lot it meant you had lots of energy. I raised my hand.

Ms. Johnson called on me. "Yes, Azaleah?"

"Are we going to set up dominoes in a fancy pattern and knock them down?" I asked.

Ms. Johnson shook her head. "Something even better," she said. "A Rube Goldberg machine is much fancier. We will use lots of different materials in the STEM lab to create a chain reaction. Your job will be to make a small bouncy ball land in a cup."

The class started to whisper about the project.

Rose leaned toward me. "I hope we're in the same group," she said.

I nodded and crossed my fingers and thumbs at Rose. "Me too," I said.

"Let's watch a Rube Goldberg machine at work," said Ms. Johnson. She turned off the lights and started a video.

Music played while a girl in the video pulled a string to start a chain reaction. I could see the energy going from one thing to another. Blocks fell over, gears spun, and a roll of toilet paper bumped a tennis ball.

The ball rolled down a path and plopped right into a garbage can. The class clapped.

"This is going to be fun!" yelled Terrance.

Ms. Johnson turned on the lights. "Now let's talk about your group assignments. I've split you up into six groups of four."

She started reading our names from a piece of paper. I waited to hear my name. Finally, she said, "Group four will be Azaleah, Rose . . ."

Rose and I grinned at each other. This was definitely turning into the best day ever!

". . . Jamal, and Terrance," finished Ms. Johnson.

My grin disappeared. I hoped Terrance wouldn't get our group in trouble with his talking.

Ms. Johnson finished reading the group assignments. "Now," she said, "let's break into our groups. You have thirty minutes."

"I thought we were going to the STEM lab," yelled Terrance.

Everyone looked at Terrance, including Ms. Johnson. She looked like she was taking three calming breaths. She had taught us to do that when we were getting upset.

"We will go tomorrow," Ms. Johnson said slowly. "We usually only go on Fridays, so I had to sign up for extra time."

Rose and I headed over to table four. I looked at the clock. Thirty minutes with talkative Terrance . . . and thirty minutes until I started my job as STEM lab monitor!

CHAPTER 3

SERIOUS BUSINESS

Our group met at table four. Rose and I sat next to each other, and Jamal sat next to Terrance.

Jamal smiled at me. I was glad he was in our group. He was very smart and worked very hard. One time Ms. Johnson let us make animal habitat dioramas. Jamal's was one of the best. He was the only one in the class who made a naked mole rat.

"This is going to be so fun," said Terrance. "I already know what our machine is going to look like."

Ms. Johnson rang the bell that meant silence, so I couldn't answer Terrance. But I wanted to. I wanted to tell him that he didn't know what our machine was going to look like because we hadn't talked about it yet. Ms. Johnson always said groups had to *discuss* ideas first.

"Here are the directions for our group planning time," Ms. Johnson said.

"We don't need time to plan," Terrance whispered to us. "We're ready to build now."

Rose and Jamal frowned. I took three calming breaths.

Ms. Johnson put chart paper up on the board. It had a list of all of the supplies in the makerspace. There were blocks, toilet paper rolls, and all kinds of other things. Then she added another piece of paper to the board.

"From now until recess, I want you to do these three things," she said.

I read the chart. It said:

Group Discussion

1. *Discuss your building ideas. Take turns speaking.*
2. *Talk about which materials you might like to use.*
3. *Work together to draw an idea of what your machine might look like.*

"Jamal, you can go first," I said. "What's your idea?"

Jamal opened his mouth, but before he could talk, Terrance did. "We are using the blocks, the racetracks, some tape, a cup, and a ball," he said.

Rose said, "I was thinking—"

Terrance interrupted. He was worse than Tiana—and she was a *major* interrupter.

"What we do," he said, "is stack the blocks and lay the tracks over them. Then the ball can roll down the track and land in the cup."

Rose's cheeks got pink. Her cheeks did that
when she laughed really hard. They also did
that when she was mad.

"We're supposed to *discuss* the idea," I said.

Rose and Jamal nodded.

Terrance said, "We don't need to. My idea
is really good."

"We should use more materials," said
Jamal. "Then we can make the machine
do different things, like in the video."

"We don't need to," said Terrance again.

Terrance reminded me of a parrot that could only say one thing.

"Read step one," I said. "Take turns speaking. That means we have to listen to *everyone's* ideas."

Jamal and Terrance looked at something behind me. I turned in my seat, and my eyes got big. The principal was standing right behind me.

"Good morning," Ms. Li said. "I thought I would visit Ms. Johnson's classroom this morning. I heard you were starting an exciting project."

My face felt hot. I wondered if my cheeks turned pink like Rose's. Ms. Li had probably heard us arguing.

Ms. Li smiled at me. "Congratulations on being the STEM lab monitor, Azaleah," she said.

I smiled back. "Thank you."

Ms. Li walked around and talked to each group. Then the morning recess bell rang, and Ms. Li left. All of the other groups handed their drawings to Ms. Johnson.

My group didn't have a drawing. My group hadn't even finished step one.

I was happy about one thing, though. It was recess. And that meant it was time for me to report for duty!

I jumped up from the table and waved goodbye to Rose. Then I fast-walked to the STEM lab. When I got there, I peeked through the door.

"Hi, Azaleah!" said Mr. Aguilar. "Come on in!"

Mr. Aguilar was one of the nicest teachers at my school. He was also very interesting. Sometimes he showed us science experiments where he mixed different liquids. They bubbled and smoked. They were called chemical reactions.

Mr. Aguilar pointed to a list on the wall. "This is the lab-monitor checklist," he said. "The top part is for morning recess. The bottom is for afternoon recess. Being the monitor is serious business. You're not just keeping the room neat and helping me set things up. You're responsible for living things."

I nodded and started following all of the steps.

1. *Give Snappy the turtle a lettuce leaf and three carrot slices from the refrigerator.*
2. *Feed the fish a tiny pinch of food.*
3. *Put one scoop of guinea pig food in Harry's dish.*
4. *Fasten the cage door!*
5. *If you have extra time, help keep the STEM lab clean.*

I saved the best—Harry the guinea pig— for last.

"Can I take Harry out of his cage?" I asked.

"Just for a minute," said Mr. Aguilar. "Make sure you close the latch and tie the string back on the door when you're done."

"Why is there a string?" I asked.

Mr. Aguilar chuckled. "Harry is a bit of an escape artist. He figured out the latch."

"Oh no," I said. "I'll be extra careful."

I picked up Harry and rubbed his fur on my face. He was the cutest little guinea pig I'd ever seen.

I gave him a very gentle guinea pig hug and kissed his head. Then I tucked him back in his cage and fastened the latch. I remembered to tie the string around the door.

When I looked up, Mr. Aguilar was watching me. "You did a really good job,

Azaleah. Thank you for being so careful with Harry."

I smiled. Being the STEM lab monitor was just as amazing as I thought it would be. I couldn't wait to hold Harry again at afternoon recess. I was going to be the best monitor Mr. Aguilar had ever seen!

* * *

I thought about Harry during writing time. I thought about Harry at lunch. I thought about Harry's cute face while Ms. Johnson read us a story. At art time, I even drew Harry.

Finally, it was afternoon recess. I ran to the STEM lab. I went to say hi to Harry right away. I put my face up to his cage, but there was a great big problem waiting for me. . . .

Harry was gone!

CHAPTER 4
HELP!

"Mr. Aguilar!" I yelled.

My eyes searched all around the lab. I didn't see Harry anywhere.

Mr. Aguilar came hurrying out of the lab storage closet. "What's wrong, Azaleah?" he asked.

I pointed to Harry's empty cage. "Harry is gone!"

"I don't believe it," Mr. Aguilar said. "He figured out the string? It must have happened while I was in the fifth-grade classroom."

I felt tears burning my eyes. *Maybe I didn't tie the string tight enough,* I thought. *What if something bad happened to Harry?*

"Where could he be?" I asked.

"Let's not panic. He can't be far," said Mr. Aguilar. "Take a look around the room. This isn't the first time Harry has escaped. I don't know how he gets down from the counter, but we always find him."

I tried to stay calm. I moved the papers and baskets and boxes that were on the counter with Harry's cage. He wasn't there.

I looked behind the blinds on the window at the end of the counter. No Harry.

I walked around the STEM lab. I looked under the shelves. I looked in the corners. I looked by the garbage can. I even looked under Mr. Aguilar's desk. I couldn't find Harry.

The bell rang. That meant recess was over. I hadn't done anything on the afternoon list.

I hadn't changed Snappy's water or put hay in Harry's cage. I hadn't put the makerspace bins away for the day either.

"Mr. Aguilar, what should I do?" I asked.

"Let's Harry-proof the room before you go," he said.

"Harry-proof?" I repeated.

Mr. Aguilar nodded. "There are things we can do to keep him safe. First, let's unplug the radio and the pencil sharpener so Harry won't chew the cords."

"Should we pick up pencils and paper scraps so Harry won't eat them?" I asked.

"Good idea, Azaleah," said Mr. Aguilar.

He helped me clean the floor. When it was time for me to leave, Mr. Aguilar locked the door.

"This way, no one can come in. And if the door is shut, Harry can't leave," explained Mr. Aguilar. "I'm sure he'll go back to his cage when he gets hungry. That's what he did last time."

I hoped Mr. Aguilar was right.

When I got back to my classroom, Rose stared at me. "Azaleah, what's wrong?" she asked. "You look scared."

I didn't want Rose to know Harry was missing. I didn't want anyone to know. They would think I was a bad STEM lab monitor.

"Nothing," I said.

During math, I did my times tables with my head on my desk. But I was so busy worrying about Harry I couldn't finish them. When it was time to go home, Ms. Johnson told me to do the rest for homework.

Mama and Tiana picked me up from school. Tiana talked about her best friend, Kevin. When we picked up Nia, she talked about her rehearsal. Mama told us about a new recipe she was trying.

The whole ride home, I stayed quiet. Nobody remembered about the STEM lab monitor announcement. I was glad because I didn't want to talk about it.

* * *

At dinner that night, I was still worrying about Harry. I must have been frowning, because Tiana stared at me.

"Azaleah, are you sad?" she asked.

Mama turned from the stove and looked at me. Daddy and Nia looked at me too.

I burst into tears. "This was the worst day ever."

"What happened?" asked Daddy.

"Oh, the STEM lab!" said Nia. "Are you sad because you didn't get picked today?"

"I *did* get picked," I cried. "But Harry escaped. HE'S MISSING! And it's all my fault!"

"The guinea pig?" asked Mama.

I nodded. "And that's not all. We started a group project. We were supposed to plan for the STEM lab tomorrow. But Terrance bossed us around and wouldn't let anybody talk," I said.

Mama handed me a napkin to wipe my face. I told my family all about my whole horrible day.

"What are you going to do?" asked Daddy.

I thought for a minute. "I'm going to find Harry," I said. "But I don't know what to do about Terrance."

"Use your words," said Tiana. "Say *NO, Terrance.* Yell *no* lots of times."

"I don't think he'll listen," I said. Plus, I knew that would start an argument.

"Pretend you're a character who solves problems," said Nia.

"I'm a real person who solves problems," I said. "But I don't know how to solve this one."

"Talk to Ms. Johnson about Terrance," said Mama.

"Talk to *Terrance* about Terrance," said Daddy. "Do it privately."

I didn't think any of those things would work. Reminders from Ms. Johnson didn't even work with Terrance.

"Can I be excused?" I asked.

My parents looked at each other. Mama nodded at me.

I spent the rest of the night alone in my bedroom. I finished my math and put on my pajamas. Then I got a book and climbed into bed. I read until Mama came to tuck me in.

She gave me a kiss and pulled my covers up to my chin. "Sleep tight," she said. "Tomorrow will be better."

I did not sleep tight. I thought about my group project. I thought about Terrance. I didn't want to tell on him. He might get mad.

I decided to use my words—but not privately. Maybe we could have a group talk. I could help Terrance listen to all of us.

But mostly I thought about poor, lost Harry. I hoped he wasn't cold. I hoped Mr. Aguilar was right and Harry would go back to his cage when he got hungry. Maybe he already had. Maybe Harry was fast asleep in his cage.

I wrapped myself in my blanket and closed my eyes. Down the hall I could hear Nia singing about the sun coming out tomorrow.

I hope she's right, I thought. Then I fell asleep.

CHAPTER 5
WORDS

When I got to school, I went straight to the STEM lab. I wanted to see if Harry was back. The door was locked. I knocked, but no one answered.

I stood there and waited. When the bell rang Mr. Aguilar still wasn't there. I had to go line up.

Rose was already standing in line. "There you are!" she said. "You're late today."

I smiled at Rose but didn't say anything. Looking at my best friend made me think about the group project. And that made me think about Terrance. I could hear his voice all the way at the back of the line.

Ms. Johnson walked us into the classroom. She waited for us to get quiet. "Today is our first day in the STEM lab," she said.

Some of the kids clapped. Terrance said, "Yesssss!"

"You will have three days to build your machines. On Friday, you will share your work with the class." Ms. Johnson pointed to the charts on the board. "Don't forget, this is group work. Take turns. Share ideas."

We lined up and went to the STEM lab. The door was unlocked, but Mr. Aguilar wasn't in there. He had put up a little screen in front of the animals, though. He did that sometimes if the lab was going to be busy. He didn't want Harry and Snappy to get scared. The problem was, I couldn't see if Harry was there.

I sighed and sat on the floor with my
group. Bins were set up all around the room.
There were building blocks and racetracks and
toilet paper rolls. There were dominoes, tape,
cups, balls, and all kinds of other things too.
There were even boards leaning against the
counter for us.

Wow! I thought. *Mr. Aguilar thought of
everything!*

"Look at all of this!" said Jamal. "We can make something really complicated."

Terrance shook his head. "It doesn't need to be complicated."

Rose said, "Let's pick our materials."

"Yeah!" said Jamal. "We didn't get to finish that part yesterday."

"I finished that part already," said Terrance. "Rose and Azaleah, you can get the tape, a cup, and a ball. Jamal and I can get the blocks and racetracks."

I could see why Tiana had told me to say, "No, Terrance." *No* was exactly what I felt like saying.

Rose, Jamal, and I looked at each other. We didn't say anything. We also didn't go get materials. This was the perfect time to use my words.

"I think we should talk about it first," I said.

Jamal and Rose nodded.

"We don't need to," Terrance said.
"We already have a plan."

Terrance was making me mad. I took three
calming breaths.

"We are supposed to share ideas," I said.

Terrance ignored me. He stood up, walked
to the bins, and got some blocks. Then he
came back and sat down.

I looked at the other groups. They were all
carrying things to their spots. Some of them
were smiling. One group had already started
building.

Rose stomped over to the bins. She got
tape, a cup, and a ball. When she came back
her cheeks were very pink.

Jamal stayed right where he was. He didn't
go get anything.

I could tell Jamal was not going to listen
to Terrance. He also was not going to use his
words.

"Jamal," said Terrance, "you forgot the racetracks."

Jamal didn't answer, so I did. "We want to tell you our ideas," I said.

"Let's just start," said Terrance. He started stacking the blocks.

I needed a break from Terrance. I headed over to the counter to peek behind the screen. I wanted to see if Harry was back.

"Azaleah!" said Terrance very loudly. "We're supposed to be working together."

I turned around. Ms. Johnson was looking at me. I frowned and went back to my group.

All around us, the other groups had started their machines. They had all kinds of materials. They were taking turns adding things to the machines. They were talking and smiling. One machine fell over. The group laughed.

Everyone is having fun but us, I thought.

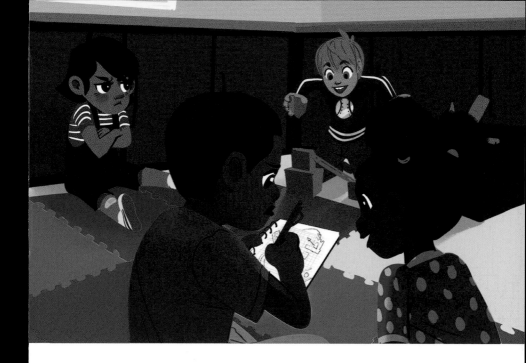

Rose rolled the ball on the floor between her hands. Jamal had gotten a piece of paper. I peeked at what he was drawing. It looked like his own plan for a Rube Goldberg machine.

Jamal's plan had really good chain reactions. It showed dominoes falling and hitting a toilet paper roll. The roll bumped over a stack of straws. He wasn't finished yet, but I liked his idea.

"That's awesome, Jamal!" I said. "Rose, look at this."

"Oh!" she said. "That's really good."

Terrance didn't even look. He kept stacking blocks and putting racetracks on top. He was talking to himself.

"First, the tracks will be on the tall blocks," he said. "Then, the stacks will get short. The tracks will go downhill. We can put the ball at the top. It will roll down and land in the cup."

"Terrance," I said, "where is the chain reaction? One thing is supposed to make another thing happen."

Rose and Jamal nodded.

"The hill is going to make the ball roll. Weren't you listening to me?" he asked.

Ms. Johnson clapped her hands. That meant it was time to stop.

Everyone lined up for morning recess except me. I needed to stay and do my STEM lab monitor job. I was glad my class was leaving. I could finally check Harry's cage.

As soon as everyone else was gone, I peeked behind the screen. Harry was still missing.

"Oh, no," I said.

I hurried over and closed the door to the lab to keep Harry inside. I fed the fish and Snappy. Then I got on my hands and knees. I crawled around on the floor.

"Harry, where are you?" I whispered. "Please come back."

I wished Mr. Aguilar would come back too. I needed help.

I didn't see any sign of Harry, but I did get an idea. If Harry was still in the lab, I should leave his food on the floor for him.

I left five pellets near Mr. Aguilar's desk. And while I was there, I spied a clue—guinea pig droppings!

Usually poop on the floor would be bad news. But not this time. This time poop was good news. It meant Harry was still in here somewhere!

CHAPTER 6

HARRY SITUATION

For the rest of the day I focused on my work. I finished my writing and had time to illustrate my story. I played two-square with Rose at lunchtime.

Finally, it was afternoon recess. When I got to the lab, Mr. Aguilar was sitting at his desk and staring at his computer.

"Hi, Azaleah," he said.

"Is Harry back?" I asked.

Mr. Aguilar's face looked a tiny bit sad and a lot stressed. "Not yet."

"Mr. Aguilar, are you okay?" I asked.

He gave me the same smile Mama did when she was extra tired. "Yes," he said. "I've just been busy getting the fifth graders ready for the D.C. Science Investigation Station. I'm a little tired."

My big sister, Nia, had done the Investigation Station in fifth grade. It was a huge contest. The fifth graders got to be science detectives. They did science investigations and solved problems. The school that won even got a trophy.

I nodded at him. "Did you see the droppings?" I asked.

Mr. Aguilar shook his head. "No! Where?"

"Right by your shoe," I said.

Mr. Aguilar looked down and nodded. He seemed happy about the poop too. "You have good eyes."

I started to clean Harry's cage. It was one of my afternoon jobs. I had to pull out the tray at the bottom and dump out the shavings. Then

I had to put in new ones. I also changed
Harry's water. Just then I observed something
interesting.

The string on Harry's cage was not untied.
It was *chewed*. This was not my fault after all!
I had been so upset yesterday I hadn't even
noticed. Harry really was an escape artist!

"Look, Mr. Aguilar." I pointed at the string.

"That little rascal," said Mr. Aguilar. "He outsmarted me again!"

I decided to do some investigating. Maybe there were other things I hadn't noticed yesterday.

I walked up and down the counter. I had to step over a Rube Goldberg machine. I noticed one of the boards from yesterday hadn't been used. It was still leaning against the counter like a ramp.

"Maybe Harry climbed down one of the boards," I said.

Mr. Aguilar rubbed his beard. "I bet you're right."

I crouched on the floor next to the end of the board. I pretended I was a guinea pig.

Where would I go? I wondered.

Since Harry's droppings were near the desk, I crawled that way. Then I found another clue!

"Mr. Aguilar, two of the food pellets I left are gone!" I exclaimed.

"You're quite the detective, Azaleah," he said. "Keep going with your investigation."

I crawled all over the room. I had to crawl around our Rube Goldberg machines very carefully. I didn't want to knock them over. Some of them were already tall. One of them had a block dangling from a string. Another one used a paper towel roll as a chute for the ball.

I didn't stop crawling until I got to the bookshelf on the other side of the room. It was a lot of work.

I bet Harry is pretty tired, I thought.

On the bottom shelf I spotted an interesting book. It was called *Raising Your Guinea Pig*. That gave me another idea.

"Mr. Aguilar, can I borrow your guinea pig book?" I asked.

I knew that scientists did lots of reading to learn new things. They called it research. Maybe I could learn something that would help me find Harry.

"Sure," he said. "The bell rang, though. You need to hurry to class."

I hadn't even heard the bell. I had been very focused on looking for clues. I took the book and stood up.

Before I left, I looked at the Rube Goldberg machines around the room. The other groups were doing a really good job.

Then I stared at ours. It was not creative. It was not complicated. There were no chain reactions. It wasn't even tall. It would not impress anyone.

I sighed. I was not close to solving the Terrance problem. Not at all. But I might be closer to solving the guinea pig mystery. And that was a good start.

CHAPTER 7
RESEARCH

That night after dinner, I ran to my room. I pulled the guinea pig book out of my backpack. I wanted to find as many clues as I could.

The first chapter was all about what guinea pigs looked like. I already knew what Harry looked like, but I read it anyway. I learned that some guinea pigs don't have fur!

The next chapter was about how to take care of a guinea pig. It was very interesting. Harry ate pellets and hay. The book said guinea pigs also liked fruits and vegetables.

I wonder if Mr. Aguilar gives Harry treats,
I thought.

That gave me a good idea. If I put out treats, maybe Harry would come get them. Then I could catch him and put him in his cage.

I grabbed a piece of paper. I started a list of guinea pig treats. I wrote:

- greens
- apples
- sweet peppers
- pears
- broccoli

I also read a very interesting fact. Guinea pigs were nocturnal. They were supposed to be awake at night. But Harry was always awake during the day.

Maybe that's because he lives in a classroom with so many visitors, I thought.

I added *nocturnal* to my paper. Then I ran back downstairs. Mama was in the kitchen chopping salt pork.

"What are you making, Mama?" I asked.

She smiled at me. "I'm making some collard greens for tomorrow."

I couldn't believe my luck! "Mama, did you know guinea pigs like collard greens?"

"No, I didn't," said Mama.

"Can I have a leaf for Harry?" I asked.

Mama handed me two big collard green leaves from a gigantic pile. I thought about my list. Greens were yummy, but apples were sweet. Harry might like apples for dessert.

I waited until Mama finished cutting the meat, so she wouldn't cut herself. Then I asked, "Mama, can you please cut me a piece of apple?"

"It's a little late for a snack, Azaleah," said Mama.

I giggled. "Not for me. For Harry!"

Mama laughed too. She cut two slices of apple for Harry. I put the greens and apples in a plastic bag. I saved them in the refrigerator for tomorrow. Then I kissed Mama and ran back to my room.

I hopped in bed with my guinea pig book. Chapter three was about guinea pig behavior. It said guinea pigs were social. They liked to be around people. They liked to play. They liked to have a nap time and a mealtime.

Maybe that's why I have to feed Harry at morning recess, I thought. *It's his mealtime.*

The book also said guinea pigs like to hide. Harry was certainly very good at that!

I had lots of good information. I also had guinea pig treats. Tomorrow, I would do some more detective work. I couldn't wait!

CHAPTER 8

CLOSED

When I got to school the next morning, I had a plan. I went straight to the STEM lab again. Mr. Aguilar was already there, taking microscopes out of a box.

"Is Harry back?" I asked.

Mr. Aguilar shook his head. "I'm starting to worry. He's never been gone this long."

I pulled out the plastic bag and held it up so Mr. Aguilar could see. "I brought treats!"

"Hmm . . . ," said Mr. Aguilar. "That's a good idea."

"Can I put them on the floor?" I asked. "Maybe Harry will come out and get them."

"Sure," said Mr. Aguilar. "I have to get my work done, so I won't be able to help this morning."

I put one leaf of greens near the desk where Harry had left droppings. Mr. Aguilar had cleaned them up. I put an apple slice near the board leaning against the counter.

The bell rang. I had to go to class. I decided to save the rest of the treats for later.

Right away, I noticed Ms. Johnson had put up a new poster. It said *Presidents and Vice Presidents of the United States*. It had a picture of every single president and vice president.

Terrance noticed it too. "Wow!" he yelled. "Where did you get that?"

Ms. Johnson said, "Don't forget to raise your hand, Terrance. Ms. Li got one of these posters for every classroom."

Terrance raised his hand. Then he talked, even though Ms. Johnson hadn't called on him. "I got to vote with my parents," he said.

I raised my hand. But I waited until Ms. Johnson called on me. When she did, I asked, "Can kids vote?"

Ms. Johnson shook her head. "Not in government elections. Only adults can vote for president. They can also vote for other leaders, like governors and mayors. Voting makes things more fair. Every vote counts."

"I didn't really vote," said Terrance. "I only watched my parents. But the people there gave me a sticker. It said *I voted.*"

"Please wait to be called on, Terrance," said Ms. Johnson. Then she said, "Azaleah, there are other ways kids can vote."

"How?" I asked.

"Let's vote right now," said Ms. Johnson. "Our turn in the STEM lab is after recess today. We are about to go out for P.E. Let's vote on what to play: kickball or basketball."

The class clapped.

"Raise your hand if you want to play basketball," said Ms. Johnson.

A few people raised their hands.

Next she said, "Raise your hand if you want to play kickball."

Most people, including me, raised their hands the second time. Kickball won.

I liked voting. It was fair.

But behind me, I heard someone say, "But I wanted to play basketball."

"Sometimes you don't win," Ms. Johnson said. "But at least your vote counted."

That gave me the most fantastic idea in the world. My group could vote about our project! We could vote to take turns sharing ideas *or* to use Terrance's idea. Plus, Terrance wouldn't even have to listen to us. He could see our hands!

* * *

I was so excited I skipped all the way to the STEM lab at morning recess. Mr. Aguilar was looking through a box on the counter. The outside said *Imagination Station*. I stood next to him and peeked into Harry's cage.

"Still no Harry?" I asked.

Mr. Aguilar let out the kind of sigh Mama did when she was extra tired. "Still no Harry," he said.

Even though there was no Harry, I had to do my other jobs. I fed Snappy and the fish. Then I decided to check the floor for more clues. First, I looked at the apple slice. It was exactly where I left it. Then, I looked at the collard green leaf.

"Mr. Aguilar!" I shouted. "Something has been nibbling at the greens! It's even moved a little bit!"

He squatted down next to me. "That's great!" he said. "While your class is in here, keep an eye out for Harry. Hopefully, he'll come back for the rest."

After the bell, my class walked into the STEM lab. Everyone sat next to their machines and got right to work.

Terrance said, "Okay, let's get the rest of the racetracks done."

I said, "I think we should take a group vote. Just like we did in class."

Rose's eyes got very big, and she nodded. Jamal grinned.

Terrance said, "We don't need—"

But before Terrance could finish, I said, "We have two choices. We can use Terrance's idea, or we can take turns and come up with a new idea."

Terrance frowned at us.

"Raise your hand for Terrance's idea," I said.

Terrance raised his hand. His frown got even bigger when we didn't raise ours.

"Raise your hand for a new group idea," I said.

I raised my hand. So did Rose and Jamal.

"But—" said Terrance.

"We voted," said Jamal.

"A new group idea won," I said.

"Sometimes you don't win," said Rose. "But at least your vote counted."

Terrance crossed his arms.

"But guess what, Terrance?" I said. "You are part of our group. You get to share ideas too."

Terrance didn't look happy, but he didn't argue. Our group took turns sharing ideas. Jamal showed us the drawing he had been working on. Rose said she wanted the ball to go through a toilet paper roll tunnel.

I said, "That's a really good idea. And I like the way Jamal's plan uses dominoes to make the ball start rolling."

Terrance said, "We can put my part at the end of Jamal's idea. The ball can go through Rose's tunnel. And then it can go down my hill."

"Oooo, and then we can make the ball fly off the cliff and into the cup!" I said.

Everyone in my group clapped. We all smiled. Even Terrance! We went to the bins together to get our materials.

On the way back to our spot, I looked around. I didn't see Harry, but I did see that some of the groups were almost done with their machines.

"We better hurry," I said. "We have to catch up and finish by tomorrow."

With everyone working together instead of arguing, we were doing a good job. Then Mr. Aguilar called me to his desk.

"Azaleah," he whispered, "have you had any luck spotting Harry?"

I shook my head. "What about you?"

"No," he admitted. "But I just got an email from Ms. Li. I mentioned this morning that Harry was missing. She wants us to close the lab until we find him."

Close the lab? I thought. *That's bad news.*

My class wouldn't be able to finish our projects. And everyone would find out that Harry was missing. Even worse, they would all know it happened while I was the monitor.

"But why do we have to close the whole lab?" I asked.

"Well, Ms. Li has to think about our health and safety," Mr. Aguilar explained. "If Harry is scared, he might bite someone."

I looked at the floor. I wished I could have just one more day in the lab. We could probably finish our project. And maybe I could find Harry too.

"I need to tell the class," said Mr. Aguilar. He walked to the front of the room. "May I have your attention, please?"

The class stopped talking and looked up. Mr. Aguilar didn't usually make announcements. Everyone waited to see what he would say.

"I have some bad news," he said. "Harry is missing."

The whole class turned and looked at me. Their eyes were big. My face got very, very hot. I hid it in my hands.

Somebody asked, "Did Azaleah lose him?" I didn't know who it was, because I couldn't see.

"No, it's not Azaleah's fault," Mr. Aguilar said. "Harry chewed through the string and let himself out. He did it when no one was looking."

All the kids started talking at the same time. Ms. Johnson clapped her hands and said, "Quiet, please."

Mr. Aguilar continued. "I have to close the lab until we find Harry. We need to keep him safe. And we need to keep you safe."

"Please stand up carefully," Ms. Johnson said. "Walk slowly to the door."

The class sadly lined up at the door. I could hear them whispering. Somebody asked, "What about our projects?"

Ms. Johnson didn't answer.

"Azaleah, please stay for a minute," said Mr. Aguilar.

Ms. Johnson led everyone out of the STEM lab. I stayed behind.

"Since the lab is closed, there's no afternoon shift today," said Mr. Aguilar.

"I'll take care of your jobs. Why don't you come back in the morning?"

I nodded. I couldn't believe the STEM lab was closed. I couldn't do my afternoon jobs. And my group couldn't finish our project, even though we had a good idea.

So much for congratulations and recognitions, I thought.

CHAPTER 9

SPECIAL PERMISSION

At dinnertime, I told my family what had happened in the STEM lab. First, I told them about voting. Then, I told them Harry was still missing.

"I'm proud of you, Azaleah," said Mama. "Voting was a good solution."

"What about Harry?" asked Tiana. "What if you never, ever find him?"

"She will," said Daddy. "Azaleah is a detective."

Daddy was right. I was a detective. And I never gave up. I *would* find Harry. But I'd have to get back into the STEM lab first.

I finished my dinner and asked, "Mama, can I use some things from the refrigerator?"

Mama nodded, so I put together a dish of fresh food for Harry. Luckily, Mama kept our refrigerator full of everything. We had all of the things on my list of favorite guinea pig foods.

I also had a fresh idea. *Maybe I need to change the way I put out the food?*

"Daddy, can you take me to school early tomorrow?" I asked.

"Why?" he asked.

"I want to do some detective work in the STEM lab," I explained.

"Will the teacher be there?" he asked.

I thought about that for a minute. "I think so. Mr. Aguilar has a lot to do. He's getting ready for the D.C. Investigation Station."

"All right," said Daddy. "Nia has rehearsal before school anyway. I can drop you off on the way."

I gave him a great big hug. Now I just had to wait until the morning.

* * *

When I got to school, the halls were still quiet. I could hear music coming from the STEM lab. That was good news.

I opened the door. Mr. Brannan was in there. He was the school custodian.

"Azaleah, you're very early," he said.

"I know. I have some work to do. Is Mr. Aguilar here?" I asked.

Mr. Brannan shook his head and emptied the small garbage can into his big garbage bag.

"Would it be okay if I come in?" I asked.

Mr. Brannan wore glasses that made his eyes look extra big. He looked at me for a long time. Then he said, "I admire hard workers. Come on in."

I went in and checked Harry's cage. He was still gone, so I got right to work. First, I crawled around on the floor. I looked for more droppings. There were some by the desk. And the collard greens were gone.

Harry was busy last night, I thought.

I took out my dish of treats. If there were fresh treats scattered all over the place, Harry would smell them. He would eat the ones that were closest. Then I could tell where he was.

Just then, Mr. Aguilar came in. He looked at Mr. Brannan, then at me. "Good morning, Azaleah," he said.

"I gave her special permission to come in," Mr. Brannan explained.

"Hi, Mr. Aguilar. I have a plan," I said.

I told him what I was doing. He nodded.

"It might work," he said. "I'll let you finish, but then you need to head on out. You aren't really supposed to be in here."

By the time school started, I had little
piles of treats in all four corners of the room.
I also put treats in the middle of the room.
There were a few piles in between our Rube
Goldberg machines too.

"See you at recess, Mr. Aguilar," I said.

"Okay," he said. "But only to check in.
The lab is still closed, remember."

I went to class, but I couldn't concentrate.
The whole time Ms. Johnson taught math,

I thought about Harry. I felt bad I hadn't found him yet.

I knew I had the right treats for him. And the guinea pig book said guinea pigs liked to be social. I couldn't figure out why Harry wasn't coming out to see me. There had to be something I wasn't thinking of.

Finally, morning recess came. This time I didn't hurry to the STEM lab. I was a little bit nervous.

What if my idea didn't work? What if Harry never comes out? I worried.

When I got there, Mr. Aguilar was waiting. "Azaleah, I really need your help. Ms. Li said it was okay. I have to get ready for a lesson. Will you please feed Snappy and the fish?" he asked.

I did what Mr. Aguilar asked me to do. Then I started checking my piles of food. The ones in the corners looked the same.

The pile in the middle looked the same too.
I started checking the piles near the Rube
Goldberg machines.

I had put three piles of food near the
projects. The first one looked the same as
it did this morning. But the second one was
almost gone!

Harry was busy last night and *this morning,*
I thought.

"Oh my goodness!" I said. "Why didn't
I think of that before?"

"Think of what?" asked Mr. Aguilar.

"Guinea pigs are nocturnal! When I was
crawling all over the STEM lab, I got tired,"
I said. "A tiny guinea pig would get *very* tired.
Especially if he was awake all night and came
out to eat during the day. I don't think Harry's
hiding from us. I think he's sleeping!"

Mr. Aguilar rubbed his beard. He leaned
forward and watched me.

I looked at the machine near the pile Harry had munched on. It was supposed to look like a castle. There was a round tower made out of blocks and a little door at the bottom.

A door just big enough for a guinea pig to crawl through, I realized.

"What if Harry is sound asleep in a Rube Goldberg machine?" I yelled.

I laid on the floor and pressed my face down. I peeked through the machine's little

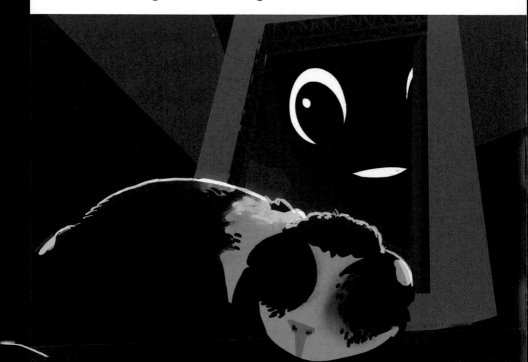

door. Inside, there was Harry, curled into a little ball. He was fast asleep.

"Harry!" I said. "There you are!"

Harry woke up and twitched his nose at me. He crawled out. I picked him up and snuggled him. I kissed his head.

"Have you been finding new cozy spots to sleep in every day?" I asked him.

"Wow, Azaleah," said Mr. Aguilar. "I didn't even see that opening. I never would have looked under there!"

"That's okay," I said. "I'm a detective. I investigate. I solve mysteries all the time."

Mr. Aguilar laughed. "You're a *scientist*! I can't wait to have you on my Investigation Station team in fifth grade. You're good!"

I put Harry back in his nice clean cage. I latched the door. I was about to tie the string around the door, but Mr. Aguilar handed me something.

"Use this wire," he said. "I don't think Harry can chew through this!"

We laughed. Harry curled back into a ball and went to sleep. He looked like he was glad to be home.

When the bell rang, Mr. Aguilar said, "Let me call Ms. Johnson. I need your help. Then maybe your class can come in."

Ms. Johnson told Mr. Aguilar it was okay for me to stay. He told her we found Harry. I could hear my class clapping and cheering all the way through the phone!

Before he hung up, he said, "You can bring the class to the lab in ten minutes. Azaleah and I need to make sure the floor is clean."

Mr. Aguilar and I checked the whole lab for droppings. We cleaned up after Harry, and Mr. Aguilar used special wipes on the floor. As soon as we finished, my class came in.

"Good job finding Harry!" said Rose.

"Yeah," said Jamal. "Thanks to you, we get to finish our project."

"I heard you had to pick up Harry's poop," said Terrance. He scrunched up his face and laughed.

"I did. But at least he's back home!" I said.

My group laughed. And then we got to work.

Ms. Johnson said we could stay all the way until lunchtime. Some of the groups finished early, and she took them outside to play. Mr. Aguilar stayed in the lab with the groups that were still working.

My group was the last one in the lab. We were still trying to get the last part of our machine to work.

"You only have five minutes left," said Mr. Aguilar.

"I'll hold the ball still," said Terrance. "Jamal, you and Azaleah get the track just right. Rose, you get the cup and put it exactly where the ball bounces."

We all took our places. Terrance let go of the ball. It rolled through the tunnel and down the hill. Rose put the cup where it landed.

"Let's run the whole machine one more time," Terrance said.

Terrance was being bossy. But he was also being a good leader. He made sure everyone had a job.

This time we tested the whole machine. Terrance tipped over the first domino. We watched the last one hit the ball. It bounced and rolled and turned and went through our machine. At the end, the ball flew off the cliff and landed right in the cup!

We all cheered and gave each other high fives. Just then, the lunch bell rang. We had finished right on time!

"Hey," I said, "we should all eat lunch together."

Terrance frowned. "Let's take a vote. Raise your hand if you want to eat together."

Then he laughed and raised his hand. So did Jamal and Rose. Mr. Aguilar laughed and said, "Let's all head out. I'm hungry too!"

CHAPTER 10

CONGRATULATIONS AND RECOGNITIONS

On Friday morning, my class was coloring pictures of fractions. The intercom chime interrupted us. It was not the normal time for Friday announcements. Friday announcements were at the end of the day. My whole class stopped to listen.

"Good morning, everyone," said Ms. Li. "Please excuse the interruption."

There was a long silence. I thought maybe Ms. Li forgot what she was going to say. But then she started talking again.

"It has been a busy week in the STEM lab," the principal said. "Ms. Johnson's class worked on a project. They learned about energy and chain reactions. I visited the lab this morning. Everyone did an excellent job on their Rube Goldberg machines. I'm very impressed."

Rose and I smiled at each other.

"I would like to recognize Ms. Johnson's third-grade class for a job well done," said Ms. Li.

"Awesome!" yelled Terrance. "She's recognizing the whole class!"

"Shhh," said Ms. Johnson. She wasn't mad, though. She was smiling.

"I tried each of your machines," Ms. Li continued. "They *all* worked! Group two, congratulations for having the tallest machine."

The kids in group two smiled at each other.

I smiled too, but I was a little disappointed. Ms. Li always did one congratulation and one recognition. That meant she was finished.

"I also have a very special congratulation and a thank you," said Ms. Li. "This week our guinea pig, Harry, went missing. Thanks to the excellent detective work of Azaleah Lane, Harry is safe and sound. He is back in his cage. Congratulations and thank you for putting so much *energy* into finding our furry friend."

My whole class clapped for me. I got a congratulation *and* a thank you.

"That's not all," said Ms. Li.

"This is a *loooonnnnng* announcement." Terrance laughed.

Ms. Li kept going. "I also happen to know that Azaleah was an excellent problem solver during the project. She should be recognized for her leadership."

My whole class cheered for me when Ms. Li finished talking. And out of everyone, Terrance cheered the loudest.

I couldn't believe it! I had gotten congratulations *and* a thank you *and* recognitions! I wondered how Ms. Li knew about our group's problem. I looked over at Ms. Johnson. She winked at me.

Without permission, Terrance got up and walked over to me. Ms. Li was still talking over the speaker. Ms. Johnson opened her mouth, and I knew Terrance was about to get a reminder.

Before Ms. Johnson could say anything, Terrance said, "Congratulations, Azaleah. You were a good problem solver. And I'm sorry I wasn't a good listener. I'll make sure everyone's vote counts next time."

Ms. Johnson closed her mouth and smiled at Terrance.

I smiled at Terrance too. "Apology accepted."

"Yay, Azaleah!" yelled Rose.

Then the whole class yelled, "Yay, Azaleah!"

I was so proud I felt like I was growing. I couldn't wait to tell Mama and Daddy.

"That is all," said Ms. Li. "Thank you for listening to the extra announcements today. Have a great weekend!"

Oh, I will, I thought. *Because I just had the best day ever!*

ABOUT THE AUTHOR

Nikki Shannon Smith is from Oakland, California, but she now lives in the Central Valley with her husband and two children. She has worked in elementary education for more than twenty-five years, and writes everything from picture books to young adult novels. When she's not busy with family, work, or writing, she loves to visit the coast. The first thing she packs in her suitcase is always a book.

ABOUT THE ILLUSTRATOR

Gloria Félix was born and raised in Uruapan, a beautiful, small city in Michoacán, Mexico. Her home is one of her biggest inspirations when it comes to art. Her favorite things to do growing up were drawing, watching cartoons, and eating, which still are some of her favorite things to do. Gloria currently lives and paints in Los Angeles, California.

GLOSSARY

chain reaction (CHAYN ree-AK-shuhn)—a series of reactions that cause more reactions of the same kind

chemical reaction (KEH-muh-kuhl ree-AK-shuhn)—a change that happens when two or more substances combine to form a new one

election (ih-LEK-shuhn)—the process of choosing someone or deciding something by voting

energy (EH-nuhr-jee)—the ability to do work, such as moving things or giving heat or light

escape artist (es-KAYP AHR-tist)—someone (such as an entertainer) who is good at escaping

monitor (MON-uh-tur)—a person who keeps track of a place or situation

nocturnal (nok-TUR-nuhl)—active at night and resting during the day

rascal (RAS-kuhl)—a mischievous person or animal

research (REE-surch)—to study and learn about a subject

Rube Goldberg machine (roob GOHLD-burg muh-SHEEN)—a machine that uses chain reactions to make something simple happen

STEM (stem)—an abbreviation for science, technology, engineering, and mathematics

vote (VOHT)—to make a choice

LET'S TALK

1. Azaleah asks her family what to do about Terrance. Mama suggests talking to the teacher. Daddy suggests talking to Terrance. Nia suggests pretending to be a character to solve the problem. Tiana says to use her words. Which advice you would have taken? Why?
2. Think about a time when you had to solve a problem. What was it? Talk about how you came up with a solution to solve it.
3. Ms. Li tells Mr. Aguilar to close the STEM lab until Harry is found. Do you agree with Ms. Li's decision? Talk about why or why not.
4. At the end of the story, Azaleah wonders how Ms. Li knew about her group's problem. How do you think Ms. Li found out? What clues from the story can you find? Talk about your ideas.

LET'S WRITE

1. Azaleah spends a lot of time trying to solve her Terrance problem. What if she had decided to write a letter to Terrance? What do you think it might say? Pretend you're Azaleah. Write a letter to Terrance to help solve the problem with the group.

2. Imagine you are Harry the guinea pig. Write a short story about your adventures while you were out of your cage. Include details from the book.

3. If your school was getting a new pet, what would you want it to be? Choose an animal, and then make a list of all of the things it would need. You might have to do some research for this one!

4. This book talks a lot about Rube Goldberg machines. But it doesn't tell you anything about Rube Goldberg! Who was he? Look up information about Rube Goldberg. Where is he from? When was he born? What was he famous for? Write a short report about Rube Goldberg. Include any interesting details and an illustration!

MAKE A RUBE GOLDBERG MACHINE!

What exactly is a Rube Goldberg machine? It is a fun machine that does a simple job. Some Rube Goldberg machines use a chain reaction to pour water. Others drop something into a cup, a can, or the garbage. There are even Rube Goldberg machines that turn off the light!

You can make a Rube Goldberg machine just like Azaleah and her group did! You can build a machine that makes a ball land in a cup, or you can make it do something different.

What You Need:

There are no rules for a Rube Goldberg machine, as long as you have permission from an adult. Here are some things you might use:

- blocks and other building materials
- boards
- cardboard
- cups
- dominoes (empty cereal boxes can be used like giant dominoes!)
- empty food cans
- foil
- magnets
- paper
- paper towel rolls
- plastic containers
- pencils
- rolls of tape
- small balls or marbles
- small weights
- string
- toilet paper rolls
- toy cars

What To Do:

1. First, decide what you want your machine to do. (There are a lot of jobs a machine can do. It can even water a plant or pop a balloon!)
2. Find a spot where you can create your machine. You might need to leave it up for a few days, so make sure it won't be in the way.
3. Gather materials for your Rube Goldberg machine.
4. Sketch a picture of your plan. (It's okay if you change materials or your plan while you're building your machine.)
5. Build your machine one part at a time and test it. If one part doesn't work, make changes.
6. After you get your machine completed, test it out.
7. Keep adjusting your Rube Goldberg machine until it works just the way you want it to!

FUN FACT: Did you know people with STEM jobs use trial and error all the time? That's what experiments are. You try something to see if it works. If it doesn't, you keep trying until you get it right. It is how we get new inventions and new medicines! It's okay if your machine doesn't work the first time. Try something, and if it doesn't work, see how you can fix it.

TIP: If you are having a really hard time, ask an adult if you can use the internet. You'll find lots of ideas and videos about Rube Goldberg machines online.

AZALEAH LANE

FINDS MYSTERY AND ADVENTURE AROUND EVERY CORNER.

CHECK OUT THE FIRST → BOOK IN THE SERIES!

DATE DUE

THE PLEASURES OF JAPANESE LITERATURE

Companions to Asian Studies
Wm. Theodore de Bary, EDITOR

DONALD KEENE ■

THE
PLEASURES
OF
JAPANESE
LITERATURE

COLUMBIA UNIVERSITY PRESS   NEW YORK

Columbia University Press
New York   Guildford, Surrey
Copyright © 1988 Columbia University Press

LIBRARY OF CONGRESS CATALOGING-IN-PUBLICATION DATA

Keene, Donald.
The pleasures of Japanese literature.

(Companions to Asian studies)
Bibliography: p.
Includes index.
1. Japanese literature—To 1868—History and
criticism. 2. Theater—Japan—History. 3. Aesthetics,
Japanese. I. Title. II. Series.
PL726.1.K44   1988   895.6'09   88-18069
ISBN 0-231-06736-4

Book design by Jennifer Dossin
Printed in the United States of America
Casebound editions of Columbia University Press books are Smyth-
sewn and are printed on permanent and durable acid-free paper

TO

SHIRLEY HAZZARD

AND

FRANCIS STEEGMULLER

CONTENTS ■

T HIS BOOK originated as five lectures, three delivered at the New York Public Library in the spring of 1986, the fourth at the University of California at Los Angeles in 1986, and the last at the Metropolitan Museum of Art in New York in 1987. Although I had at first intended to discuss all periods of Japanese literature and theater, I discovered that I really wanted to talk about traditional, rather than modern developments. The present book, which grew out of the lectures, is therefore concerned with the Japanese poetry, prose, and drama of the premodern eras, and only passing references are made to the achievements of recent times.

The lectures—and this book—were intended for a general audience, and certain information well known to every scholar of Japan was included for this reason. I have added a list of suggested readings for persons who wish to go beyond this introduction to more detailed studies and to the works that have been translated into English.

THE FIRST of the four illustrations that follow shows the poet Ono no Komachi as depicted in the scroll *Nyōbō Sanjūrokunin Uta-awase* (Thirty-six Women Poets, Their Poems Compared) by the eighteenth-century painter Minamoto no Nobuyoshi. The text is typical of the melancholy passion of her poems: "I realize now that the thing that fades, its color invisible, is the flower in the heart of one who lives in this world."

The second is an illustration by the seventeenth-century artist Tawaraya Sōtatsu for a section of *Tales of Ise*. It portrays Narihira journeying to the east, disappointed by life at the court. On the way he meets an acquaintance who is returning to the capital, and he gives the man a message for a woman he has left behind: "Here by Mount Utsu in Suruga, I do not meet you, alas, neither in reality or even in dreams."

The third is an illustration by the seventeenth-century painter Chōjirō of a scene from the Tamakazura (The Jew-

eled Chaplet) chapter of *The Tale of Genji*. It shows Genji
offering presents of New Year's robes to the various ladies
who live in his palace.

The last is a sketch by Kawanabe Gyōsai (1831–1889) of a
scene from the Kabuki play *Meiboku Sendai Hagi*, first
performed in 1777. The complicated plot includes a scene in
which a huge rat, cornered by men loyal to the rightful heir
to the domain, reveals his true appearance, a man in gray
carrying the same scroll that the rat had in its mouth.
Members of the audience are visible on the other side of the
trapdoor through which the rat disappears.

■ CREDITS

The *Nyōbō Sanjūrokunin Uta-awase* illustration by Minamoto
no Nobuyoshi (mid-eighteenth century, Edo period; handscroll,
ink, gold, and color on paper) appears courtesy of the Spencer
Collection, The New York Public Library; Astor, Lenox and
Tilden Foundations.

The Tawaraya Sōtatsu illustration of the Mount Utsu episode
from the *Tales of Ise* (seventeenth century, Edo period; hanging
scroll, color and gold on paper) and the Chōjiro illustration of
the Jeweled Chaplet chapter of *The Tale of Genji* (end of sixteenth–early seventeenth century: hanging scroll, color on paper) appear courtesy of the Mary and Jackson Burke Collection
New York, New York; photos by Otto E. Nelson.

The sketch by Kawanabe Gyōsai of a scene from the Kabuki
play *Meiboku Sendai Hagi* (Meiji period; 75.29-12 Japanese
Drawing; 25.3 x 36.5 cm) appears courtesy of the Freer Gallery
of Art, Smithsonian Institute, Washington, D.C.

女房三十六人歌合

尼　　小野小町

色みえて
うつろふものは
世の中の
人の心の
花にぞありける

THE PLEASURES OF JAPANESE LITERATURE

JAPANESE
AESTHETICS

IT WOULD BE difficult to describe adequately in the course of a few pages the full range of Japanese aesthetics or even to suggest the main features of Japanese taste as it has evolved over the centuries. It probably would be even more difficult to discuss any aspect of Japanese culture without alluding to the Japanese sense of beauty, perhaps the central element in all of Japanese culture. I will attempt to describe some of the characteristics of Japanese taste in terms of one book, *Tsurezuregusa* (Essays in Idleness), a collection of short essays by the priest Kenkō, written mainly between 1330 and 1333. This work does not explain the whole of Japanese aesthetics, obviously not the developments of the last six hundred years, but I believe that it contains much that illuminates Japanese preferences today, despite the long interval of time since it was written and despite the immense changes that Japanese civilization has undergone, especially during the past century.

The author is generally known by his name as a Buddhist

priest, Kenkō. His name when he was born in 1283 was Urabe no Kaneyoshi, and he came from a family of hereditary Shintō priests. It is somewhat surprising that a man of a Shintō background should have become a Buddhist, but the two religions of Japan, though antithetical in many respects, were both accepted by the Japanese; in general, the Japanese in the past (and the present) have turned to Shintō for help in this life, and to Buddhism for salvation in the world to come.

Kenkō, though his rank as a Shintō priest was modest, seems to have won a secure place in court circles thanks to his skill at composing poetry. This alone should suggest how highly poetic skill was valued by the court, which in most respects was acutely conscious of rank and ancestry. For courtiers, an ability to compose poetry was an indispensable accomplishment, and Kenkō may have been welcomed to the palace less as a poet than as a tutor in poetry to those who lacked outstanding poetic talent.

Kenkō took Buddhist orders in 1324 at the age of 41, after the death of the Emperor Go-Uda, whom he had served. Many reasons have been adduced for his decision to "leave the world," but nothing in his writings suggests that it was an act of despair. Buddhist thought figures prominently in *Essays in Idleness,* and it can hardly be doubted that Kenkō was sincere when he urged readers to "flee from the Burning House" of this world and find refuge in religion. But he did not in the least resemble the typical Buddhist monks of the medieval period, who either lived in monasteries or else were hermits. Kenkō lived in the city and was as familiar with worldly gossip as with Buddhist doctrine. Certain Buddhist beliefs, notably the impermanence of all things, run through his work, but even though he insisted that the possessions that people accumulate in this world do not last,

he did not condemn them as hateful dross, as a more ortho-
dox Buddhist priest might have. Obviously, he did not reject
the world. Ultimately this world was not enough, but Kenkō
seems always to be saying that while we are here we should
try to enrich our lives with beauty.

Essays in Idleness consists of 243 sections. They are not
systematically presented; it was in the nature of a work in
the *zuihitsu* tradition of "following the brush," to allow
one's writing brush to skip from one topic to another in
whichever direction it was led by free association. Kenkō did
not enunciate a consistent philosophy—it is easy to find
contradictions among the various sections, and some are so
trivial in content that we may wonder why he included
them. But a concern with beauty is never far from his
thoughts, and this aspect of the work, much more than its
Buddhist message, has influenced Japanese taste. *Essays in
Idleness* was unknown to the reading public during Kenkō's
lifetime, but it came into prominence at the beginning of the
seventeenth century, and since then has been one of the best
known of the Japanese classics. Kenkō's tastes at once reflected those of Japanese of much earlier times, and greatly
contributed to the formation of the aesthetic preferences of
Japanese for centuries to come.

A typical section of *Essays in Idleness* will illustrate Kenkō's
manner. It is section 81.

A screen or sliding door decorated with a painting or
inscription in clumsy brushwork gives an impression less
of its own ugliness than of the bad taste of the owner. It is
all too apt to happen that a man's possessions betray his
inferiority. I am not suggesting that a man should own
nothing but masterpieces. I refer to the practice of deliberately decorating in a tasteless and ugly manner 'to keep

the house from showing its age,' or adding all manner of useless things in order to create an impression of novelty, though only producing an effect of fussiness. Possessions should look old, not overly elaborate; they need not cost much, but their quality should be good.[1]

Some years ago, when writing an essay on Japanese tastes, I chose four characteristics that seemed to me of special importance: suggestion, irregularity, simplicity, and perishability. These still seem to me to be a valid way to approach the Japanese sense of beauty, though I am fully aware that they do not cover everything. Generalizations are always risky. If, for example, one says of the Nō drama that it is a crystallization of Japanese preferences for understatement, muted expression, and symbolic gesture, how is one to explain why the Japanese have also loved Kabuki, which is characterized by larger-than-life poses, fierce declamation, brilliant stage effects, and so on? The clean lines of the Katsura Palace are today recognized everywhere as representative of the essence of Japanese architecture, but it was a European who first described the beauty of the palace in writings published in the 1930s, and Japanese over the centuries have usually praised instead the garishly decorated mausoleum of the shoguns at Nikkō, built about the same time.

Again, I feel quite sure that no people are more sensitive to beauty than the Japanese, but one Japanese critic, Sakaguchi Ango, wrote in 1942, "A more convenient life is more important to the Japanese than the beauty of tradition or of the authentic Japanese appearance. Nobody would be

1. *Essays in Idleness: The Tsurezuregusa of Kenkō*, Donald Keene, trans. (New York: Columbia University Press, 1967), p. 70. All subsequent quotations from this work are from this edition.

discomforted if all the temples in Kyoto and Buddhist stat-
ues in Nara were completely destroyed, but we would certainly be inconvenienced if the streetcars stopped running."
Sakaguchi was being cynical, but there is more than a grain
of truth in what he wrote, and it took some courage to
publish such ideas in 1942, at a time when the Japanese were
otherwise asserting the spiritual superiority of their culture.
With these cautions in mind, I would like to discuss the four
aspects of Japanese taste I noted above, referring particularly
to Kenko's opinions in *Essays in Idleness*.

■ SUGGESTION

The most eloquent expression of Kenkō's advocacy of suggestion as an aesthetic principle is found in section 137.

> Are we to look at cherry blossoms only in full bloom,
> the moon only when it is cloudless? To long for the moon
> while looking on the rain, to lower the blinds and be
> unaware of the passing of the spring—these are even more
> deeply moving. Branches about to blossom or gardens
> strewn with faded flowers are worthier of our admiration.
> . . . People commonly regret that the cherry blossoms
> scatter or that the moon sinks in the sky, and this is
> natural; but only an exceptionally insensitive man would
> say, "This branch and that branch have lost their blos-
> soms. There is nothing worth seeing now."
> In all things, it is the beginnings and ends that are
> interesting. Does the love between men and women refer
> only to the moments when they are in each other's arms?
> The man who grieves over a love affair broken off before
> it was fulfilled, who bewails empty vows, who spends long
> autumn nights alone, who lets his thoughts wander to

distant skies, who yearns for the past in a dilapidated house
—such a man truly knows what love means.

The moon that appears close to dawn after we have long
waited for it moves us more profoundly than the full moon
shining cloudless over a thousand leagues. And how incomparably lovely is the moon, almost greenish in its
light, when seen through the tops of the cedars deep in the
mountains, or when it hides for a moment behind cluster-
ing clouds during a sudden shower! The sparkle on hickory
or white-oak leaves seemingly wet with moonlight strikes
one to the heart. . . .

And are we to look at the moon and the cherry blossoms
with our eyes alone? How much more evocative and pleasing it is to think about the spring without stirring from the
house, to dream of the moonlight though we remain in
our room!

Kenkō presents his views so compellingly that we may
assent without noticing that they contradict commonly held
Western views on the same subjects. The Western ideal of
the climactic moment—when Laocoön and his sons are caught
in the terrible embrace of the serpent, when the soprano hits
high C, or when the rose is in full bloom—grants little
importance to the beginnings and ends. The Japanese have
also been aware of the appeal of climactic moments: they
celebrate the full moon far more often than the crescent, and
the radio breathlessly informs listeners when the cherry
blossoms will be in full bloom, not when they are likely to
scatter. But although the Japanese share with other peoples
a fondness for flowers in full bloom, their love of the barely
opened buds and of fallen blossoms is distinctive. The Japanese
seem to have been aware that the full moon (or the full
flowering of a tree), however lovely, blocks the play of the

imagination. The full moon or the cherry blossoms at their peak do not suggest the crescent or the buds (or the waning moon and the strewn flowers), but the crescent and the buds do suggest full flowering. Beginnings that suggest what is to come, or ends that suggest what has been, allow the imagination room to expand beyond the literal facts to the limits of the capacities of the reader of a poem, the spectator at a Nō play, or the connoisseur of a monochrome painting.

Kenkō did not create the preference for beginnings and ends that he describes, but he was probably the first to state it as a principle. We find a similar phenomenon in earlier collections of Japanese poetry, though no one ever explained the reason. The innumerable love poems preserved in anthologies of Japanese poetry almost never express the joy of meeting the beloved; instead, they convey the poet's yearning for a meeting, or else his—or more commonly, her— sorrow at the realization that an affair is over and there will not be another meeting.

In Japanese painting, especially of the period when Kenkō was writing, the use of suggestion is carried to great lengths, a few brush strokes serving to suggest ranges of mountains, or a single stroke a stalk of bamboo. A desire to suggest rather than to state in full was surely behind the preference for ink paintings. No people has a surer sense of color than the Japanese, and there are many splendid Japanese works of art in brilliant colors; but in the medieval period especially, many painters renounced color in favor of monochromes. I have never seen any reason stated for this preference, but I wonder whether it was not dictated also by an awareness of the power of suggestion. A mountain painted in green can never be any other color but green, but a mountain whose outlines are given with a few strokes of black ink can be any color. To add even the most delicate colors to a monochrome would be as disconcerting as adding color to Greek marbles, or in as bad taste as the rubies and emeralds with which the sultans decorated their Chinese porcelains.

■ IRREGULARITY

A second notable characteristic of Japanese taste is irregularity, and once again I turn to Kenkō for an illustrative passage. In section 82 he says, "In everything, no matter what it may be, uniformity is undesirable. Leaving something incomplete makes it interesting, and gives one the feeling that there is room for growth. Someone once told me, 'Even when building the imperial palace, they always leave one place unfinished.' " Kenkō gave an example of what he meant: "People often say that a set of books looks ugly if all volumes are not in the same format, but I was impressed to hear the Abbot Kōyū say, 'It is typical of the unintelligent man to insist on assembling complete sets of everything. Imperfect sets are better.' " I doubt that many librarians would agree with the Abbot Kōyū, but anyone who has ever faced a complete set of the Harvard Classics or any similar series knows how uninviting it is.

The Japanese have been partial not only to incompleteness but to another variety of irregularity, asymmetry. This is one respect in which they differ conspicuously from the Chinese and other peoples of Asia. In ancient (and modern) Iranian art there is often a tree in the center of the picture or pattern with beasts on either side. If a line is drawn vertically through the tree, what is on the right side is likely to be a mirror image of what is on the left. One finds symmetry also in Chinese art and architecture, though it is not quite so rigid. The typical plan of a Chinese monastery has the same buildings on one side of a central axis as on the other. But in Japan, even when the original plan called for symmetry along Chinese lines, it did not take long for the buildings to cluster, seemingly of their own volition, on one side or the other.

In literary style, parallelism in poetry and prose is a staple feature of Chinese expression. Japanese writing that is not specifically under Chinese influence avoids parallelism, and the standard verse forms are in irregular numbers of lines— five for the *tanka*, three for the *haiku*. This is in marked contrast to the quatrains that are typical poetic forms not only in China but throughout most of the world.

We find the same tendency in calligraphy, too. The Japanese, ever since they acquired skill in writing Chinese characters, have excelled in "grass writing," the cursive script, but there are few outstanding examples of the more formal style of calligraphy, which the Japanese happily leave to the Chinese. Japanese children are taught in calligraphy lessons never to bisect a horizontal stroke with a vertical one: the vertical stroke should always cross the horizontal one at some point not equidistant from both ends. A symmetrical character is considered to be "dead." The writing most admired by the Japanese tends to be lopsided or at any rate highly individual, and copybook perfection is admired only with condescension.

Irregularity is also a feature of Japanese ceramics, especially those varieties that are most admired by the Japanese themselves. The Bizen or Shigaraki wares that are the delight of connoisseurs are almost never regular in shape. Some of the finest examples are lopsided or bumpy, and the glaze may have been applied in such a way as to leave bald patches here and there. A roughness caused by tiny stones in the clay is also much admired. These would be serious faults if the potter had intended to make a bowl or jar in a symmetrical shape with an even glaze and failed, but that was clearly not his aim. The Japanese have produced flawless examples of porcelain, and these too are admired, but they are not much loved. Their perfection, especially their regularity, seems to repel the hands of the person who drinks tea from them, and flowers arranged in porcelain vases seem to be challenged rather than enhanced.

Irregularity is present too in flower arrangements (notably those based on "heaven, earth, and man") and in gardens. The gardens at Versailles, with their geometrical precision, would hardly have struck the Japanese of the past as a place for relaxation. The celebrated Japanese gardens insist on irregularity as determinedly as the classical European gardens insisted on symmetry. One European authority on gardens, D. P. Clifford, expressed in *A History of Garden Design* (1963) his distaste for the famous sand and stone garden of the Ryōan-ji, in these terms:

> It is the logical conclusion of the refinement of the senses, the precipitous world of the abstract painter, a world in which the stains on the cover of a book can absorb one more utterly than the ceiling of the Sistine Chapel; it is the narrow knife edge of art, overthrowing and discarding all that man has ever been and achieved in favour of some mystic contemplative ecstasy, a sort of suspended explosion of the mind, the dissolution of identity. You really cannot go much further than this unless you sit on a cushion like Oscar Wilde and contemplate the symmetry of an orange.

The symmetry of an orange was hardly likely to absorb the attention of the architects of this exceedingly asymmetrical garden, and far from being artless "stains on the cover of a book," the Ryōan-ji garden is the product of a philo-

sophical system—that of Zen Buddhism—as serious as the
one that inspired the ceiling of the Sistine Chapel. And, it
might be argued, even a European might derive great pleasure from daily contemplation of the fifteen stones of the
Ryōan-ji garden, without "overthrowing and discarding all
that man has ever been and achieved." The Sistine Chapel
is magnificent, but it asks our admiration rather than our
participation; the stones of the Ryōan-ji, irregular in shape
and position, allow us to participate in the creation of the
garden, and thus may move us even more. But that may be
because in our age, Western artistic expression is closer to
that of the Ryōan-ji than to that of Michelangelo.

■ SIMPLICITY

Kenkō has much to say about the third characteristic of
Japanese aesthetics that I would like to discuss, simplicity. I
will quote a few of his views, from section 10 of *Essays in
Idleness:*

> A house, I know, is but a temporary abode, but how
> delightful it is to find one that has harmonious proportions
> and a pleasant atmosphere. One feels somehow that even
> moonlight, when it shines into the quiet domicile of a
> person of taste, is more affecting than elsewhere. A house,
> though it may not be in the current fashion or elaborately
> decorated, will appeal to us by its unassuming beauty—a
> grove of trees with an indefinably ancient look; a garden
> where plants, growing of their own accord, have a special
> charm; a verandah and an open-work wooden fence of
> interesting construction; and a few personal effects left
> lying about, giving the place an air of having been lived in.
> A house which multitudes of workmen have polished with

every care, where strange and rare Chinese and Japanese furnishings are displayed, and even the bushes and trees of the garden have been trained unnaturally, is ugly to look at and most depressing. How could anyone live for long in such a place?

Kenkō expresses himself so well that we are likely to agree, perhaps a little too easily; houses which multitudes of workmen have polished with every care have generally been considered very desirable, as we know from old photographs showing the profusion of treasures with which the drawing rooms of the rich used to be adorned. Gardens where even the bushes and trees have been trained unnaturally still attract visitors to the great houses of Europe. Kenkō asks rhetorically "how could anyone live for long in such a place?" but generations of Europeans and even some Americans seem to have had no trouble.

Perhaps Kenkō would answer this with another passage from *Essays in Idleness:* "It is excellent for a man to be simple in his tastes, to avoid extravagance, to own no possessions, to entertain no craving for wordly success. It has been true since ancient days that wise men are rarely rich" (section 18). Kenkō's professed dislike for possessions may stem from Buddhist convictions. Elsewhere in his book he states it even more strongly:

The intelligent man, when he dies, leaves no possessions. If he has collected worthless objects, it is embarrassing to have them discovered. If the objects are of good quality, they will depress his heirs at the thought of how attached he must have been to them. It is all the more deplorable if the possessions are ornate and numerous. If a man leaves possessions, there are sure to be people who will quarrel disgracefully over them, crying, *"I'm getting that one!"* If

JAPANESE AESTHETICS   15

you wish something to go to someone after you are dead, you should give it to him while you are still alive. Some things are probably indispensable to daily life, but as for the rest, it is best not to own anything at all. (section 140)

Obviously, however, people have to live in houses of some sort, and Kenkō, for all his insistence on simplicity, was certainly not urging people to live in hovels. Here is how he described the kind of house he liked: "A house should be built with the summer in mind. In winter it is possible to live anywhere, but a badly made house is unbearable when it gets hot. . . . People agree that a house which has plenty of spare room is attractive to look at and may be put to many uses" (section 55).

Kenkō's prescription has been followed by many Japanese, as anyone who has spent a winter in a Kyoto house knows. When the Japanese settled Hokkaidō in the late nineteenth century they still went on building with the summer in mind, and quietly froze in the winter. But leaving aside the matter of temperature, Kenkō's insistence on having plenty of spare room has typified Japanese houses at their most artistic. It is easy too for us to accept the principle that it is better to have too little rather than too much furniture; we have been trained to believe that "less is more," but this was not true of people at the beginning of this century.

It is by no means inexpensive to build a Japanese house of the kind Kenkō favored. Simplicity is probably more expensive than ornateness, a luxury concealing luxury. Walls decorated with gilt cupids can be repainted or regilded from time to time, and the wood need not be absolutely first-rate; but the unpainted wood of the *tokonoma* cannot be so easily disguised. The Japanese preference for unpainted wood is today much admired abroad and even imitated, but it was not so in the past. When the distinguished British diplomat and author Harold Nicolson visited Kyoto early in this century he remarked that it looked like a town in the Wild West, presumably because the exteriors of the buildings were not painted; and more recently, during the Occupation, it is said that Americans painted the woodwork to brighten the houses they occupied.

Simplicity as an aesthetic principle is, of course, not confined to houses and their furnishings. Perhaps the most extreme example of the Japanese love for unobtrusive elegance is the tea ceremony. The ideal sought by the great teamaster Sen no Rikyū (1522–1591) was *sabi*, related to the word *sabi*, for "rust," or *sabireru*, "to become desolate." This may seem like a curious aesthetic ideal, but it was perhaps a reaction to parvenu extravagance in an age when military men obtained sudden power and wealth. Rikyū's sabi was not the enforced simplicity of the man who could not afford better, but a refusal of easily obtainable luxury, a preference for a rusty-looking kettle to one of gleaming newness. The tea ceremony is sometimes attacked today as a perversion of the ideal of simplicity. The prized utensils are by no means ordinary wares but may cost fortunes. But the spending of a great deal of money in order to achieve an appearance of bare simplicity is quite in keeping with Japanese tradition.

The Portuguese missionary João Rodrigues (1561–1633) described with admiration a tea ceremony he had attended, but he could not restrain his astonishment over the lengths to which the Japanese carried their passion for unobtrusive luxury:

> Because they greatly value and enjoy this kind of gathering to drink tea, they spend large sums of money in building such a house, rough though it may be, and in purchasing

the things needed for drinking the kind of tea which is offered in these meetings. Thus there are utensils, albeit of earthenware, which come to be worth ten, twenty or thirty thousand *cruzados* or even more—a thing which will appear as madness and barbarity to other nations that know of it.[2]

Madness perhaps, but surely not barbarity! The avoidance of a display of conspicuous wealth, regardless of how much the objects actually cost, is typical of the Japanese insistence on simplicity. But surely it would be far more barbarous to calculate the value of objects solely in the terms of typical European collectors of exotic bric-a-brac: how many workmen have gone blind to make them?

One more example of the Japanese preference for simplicity is found in Japanese food, and not only the variety served in connection with a tea ceremony. Japanese food lacks the intensity of flavor found in the cuisines of other countries of Asia. Spices are seldom used, garlic almost never. Just as the faint perfume of the plum blossom is preferred to the heavy odor of the lily, the barely perceptible differences in flavor between different varieties of raw fish are prized and paid for extravagantly. The taste of natural ingredients, not tampered with by sauces, is the ideal of Japanese cuisine; and the fineness of a man's palate is often tested by his ability to distinguish between virtually tasteless dishes of the same species. The early European visitors to Japan, though they praised almost everything else, had nothing good to say about Japanese food. Bernardo de Avila Girón wrote, "I will not praise Japanese food for it is not good, albeit it is pleasing to the eye, but instead I will describe the clean and peculiar way in which it is served." His judgment was re-

2. Quoted in Michael Cooper, *They Came to Japan* (Berkeley: University of California Press, 1965), p. 265.

peated by foreign visitors for the next three hundred years. The current popularity of Japanese food may be another sign of the general trend I have already mentioned towards a congruence of contemporary American and traditional Japanese tastes.

■ PERISHABILITY

The last of the four qualities of Japanese aesthetic preference that I have chosen to describe is the most unusual, perishability. In the West, permanence rather than perishability has been desired, and this has led men to build monuments of deathless marble. The realization that even such monuments crumble—proof of the inexorability of the ravages of time—has led men since the age of the Greeks to reflect on the uncertainty of the world.

Lafcadio Hearn (1850–1904), a widely-read popularizer of Japanese landscapes and customs, wrote in *Kokoro* (1896):

> Generally speaking, we construct for endurance, the Japanese for impermanency. Few things for common use are made in Japan with a view to durability. The straw sandals worn out and replaced at each stage of a journey; the robe consisting of a few simple widths loosely stitched together for wearing, and unstitched again for washing; the fresh chopsticks served to each new guest at a hotel; the light *shōji* frames serving at once for windows and walls, and repapered twice a year; the mattings renewed every autumn,—all these are but random examples of countless small things in daily life that illustrate the national contentment with impermanency.

Hearn's comments were astute, but it might be even more accurate to say that the Japanese have not only been content with impermanency, but have eagerly sought it. Once more, a passage from Kenkō helps to illuminate this traditional preference:

Somebody once remarked that thin silk was not satisfactory as a scroll wrapping because it was so easily torn. Ton'a replied, "It is only after the silk wrapper has frayed at top and bottom, and the mother-of-pearl has fallen from the roller that a scroll looks beautiful." This opinion demonstrated the excellent taste of the man. (section 82)

Signs of wear and tear such as the fraying of a silk wrapper or the loss of mother-of-pearl inlay from the roller would probably dismay most other people, and it is likely that the owner would send for a restorer, but in Japan an object of such perfection, such gleaming newness that it might have been made yesterday has seemed less desirable than a work that has passed through many hands and shows it. Such an object acquires the mysterious quality that, according to Robert Graves in a lecture I once heard, is called *barak* by the Arabs. Even a typewriter one has banged at for thirty years acquires barak because one has grown to know and perhaps even to love its little eccentricities; how much more true this is of a work of art, whose flaws are sometimes as attractive as its intrinsic beauty. A pottery bowl that has been cracked and mended, not invisibly but with gold, as if to call attention to the cracks, is human, suggesting the long chain of people who have held it in their hands—more human than a bowl that looks as if it might have been made very recently. The common Western craving for objects in mint condition, that look as if they were painted or sculpted the day before, tends to deprive antiques of their history; the Japanese prize the evidence that a work of art has been held in many hands.

Western traditions seem to go back to the Greeks, who

constantly bewailed the uncertainty of fate and insisted that no man should be called happy until he was dead, lest cruel Nemesis catch up with him. The Japanese were perhaps the first to discover the special pleasure of impermanence, and Kenkō especially believed that impermanence was a necessary element in beauty. He wrote early in *Essays in Idleness*, "If man were never to fade away like the dews of Adashino, never to vanish like the smoke over Toribeyama, but lingered on forever in this world, how things would lose their power to move us! The most precious thing in life is its uncertainty." The frailty of human existence, a common theme in the literature of the world, has probably not been recognized elsewhere than in Japan as a necessary condition of beauty. This may explain the fondness for building temples of wood, even though stronger materials were available: the very signs of aging that made Harold Nicolson recall the wooden buildings of frontier towns give greater aesthetic pleasure to the Japanese than age-repellent walls of brick or stone.

The special love the Japanese have for cherry blossoms is surely also connected with the appreciation of perishability. Cherry blossoms are lovely, it is true, but not so lovely as to eclipse totally the beauty of peach blossoms or plum blossoms. But the Japanese plant cherry trees wherever they can, even in parts of the country whose climate is not suitable for these rather delicate trees. Several years ago I visited Hirosaki in the north of Japan, a town known for its huge apple orchards. When I went to buy postcards I discovered not one that showed apple blossoms, but many devoted to cherry blossoms, which, though lovely, are hardly unique to Hirosaki. Perhaps the greatest attraction of the cherry blossoms is not their intrinsic beauty but their perishability: plum blossoms remain on the boughs for a month or so, and other fruit trees have blossoms for at least a week, but cherry blossoms normally fall after a brief three days of flowering, a fact that countless poets have had occasion to lament. Ornamental cherry trees do not produce edible fruit and they attract caterpillars and other disagreeable insects, so many that it is wise to carry an umbrella when passing under them in the late summer; but the Japanese happily plant these trees wherever they can, for their three days of glory.

Japanese when traveling abroad are sometimes startled by the indifference of people in the West to the passage of time in nature. The tea master Rikyū is said to have scattered a few leaves over a garden path that had recently been swept, in order to give it a natural look and to emphasize the sense of process; and the great novelist Natsume Sōseki, when traveling in Europe at the beginning of this century, was struck by the insensitivity of Europeans to the beauty of the changes effected by nature. He wrote,

> When I was in England, I was once laughed at because I invited someone for snow-viewing. At another time I described how deeply the feelings of Japanese are affected by the moon, and my listeners were only puzzled. . . . I was invited to Scotland to stay at a palatial house. One day, when the master and I took a walk in the garden, I noted that the paths between the rows of trees were all thickly covered with moss. I offered a compliment, saying that these paths had magnificently acquired a look of age. Whereupon my host replied that he intended soon to get a gardener to scrape all this moss away.[3]

3. Translated by Matsui Sakako, in *Natsume Sōseki as a Critic of English Literature* (Tokyo: Centre for East Asian Cultural Studies, 1975), p. 34.

Natsume Sōseki was a novelist, that is, a man who invented stories as his career, so we need not take his anecdote as literal truth. But it is unquestionable that Sōseki responded more to snow-viewing, the moon, and gardens with mossy paths than to herbaceous borders or avenues of carefully trimmed evergreens. He was heir to tastes that had evolved in Japan over many centuries, partly under the influence of Kenkō's writings. Sōseki had also read a great deal of English literature and possessed a remarkable store of knowledge concerning such varied authors as Shakespeare, Laurence Sterne, and George Meredith, but apparently at the most fundamental level, the level of his appreciation of beauty, concepts other than those he found in Western books still dominated.

The Western visitor to Japan today who expects to find exquisite beauty wherever he looks is likely to be disappointed and even shocked by his first encounters with contemporary culture. He will notice Kentucky Fried Chicken establishments and other fast-food shops, the ugliness of commercial signs, the blank looks on the faces of people hurrying to places of business that more clearly resemble contemporary models in the West than anything traditional. But the past survives in aesthetic preferences that often find surprising outlets for expression—a box of sushi, a display of lacquered zori, branches of artificial maple leaves along a commercial street. And the man who prides himself on his elegantly tailored Western clothes will be delighted to sit in Japanese style, destroying the creases, at a restaurant where traditional food is served with traditional elegance. The Japanese aesthetic past is not dead. It accounts for the magnificent profusion of objects of art that are produced each year, and its principles, the ones I have described, are not forgotten even in an age of incessant change.

TWO

JAPANESE
POETRY

IN A TEMPLE in Shimane Prefecture, the old land of Izumo, there is a monument proclaiming that this was the birthplace of Japanese poetry. I cannot recall having heard of a similar monument for English, French, or Italian poetry. The monument declares that long, long ago, in the age of the gods, within the grounds of this very temple, the god Susanoo composed the first poem recorded in the *Kojiki* (Record of Ancient Matters). The *Kojiki*, the oldest Japanese book, was presented to the court in A.D. 712. Some Japanese take this inscription as literal truth, even today when much doubt has been thrown on the account of the ancient past found in the *Kojiki*, but most scholars believe it highly improbable that the very first poem could have been written in the regular form of a waka, for over a millennium the most typical form of Japanese poetry. Other poems in the *Kojiki* are incantations whose meaning is obscure, or else poems with lines of irregular length and no discernible poetic form. Probably Susanoo's poem (assuming that a god,

rather than a mere mortal actually composed it) was re-
phrased at some time in the past to make it fit its present,
regular form. Even in its present form the content is primitive, but it makes a suitable starting point for a discussion of
Japanese poetry.

> *yakumo tatsu*
> *Izumo yaegaki*
> *tsumagomi ni*
> *yaegaki tsukuru*
> *sono yaegaki wo*

> Eightfold rising clouds
> Build an eightfold fence
> An eightfold Izumo fence
> Wherein to keep my bride—
> Oh, splendid eightfold fence![1]

Scholars have interpreted this poem variously as a mar-
riage song, a work song sung when building a new house, or
as a ritual song invoking the protection of the Izumo gods
for a newly wed couple. The poem is notable, as I have
indicated, because it exactly observes the metrics of what
would become the classical verse form, known at different
times as *uta*, *waka*, or *tanka*, thirty-one syllables arranged
in five lines of five, seven, five, seven, and seven syllables.
The repetition of phrases, typical of primitive poetry but
most uncommon in later waka, lends the rhythm of an
incantation, as does the insistence on the number eight *(ya)*,
used to signify any large number. The first line, which
means literally "eight clouds rise," is a *makurakotoba*, or
"pillow-word," a fixed epithet placed before the names of

---

1. My translation. Throughout the book, where no citation is given,
translations are my own.

provinces, mountains, and certain other nouns, and perhaps intended originally to invoke the magic of a place by mentioning its special attribute—its title, as it were. It is rather like the epithets found in Homer, such as "ox-eyed Hera" or "fleet-footed Achilles," used even when the eyes or feet of the person are not in question. *Yakumo tatsu* (eight clouds rise) was the makurakotoba for Izumo, a region on the Japan Sea coast. The name "Izumo" was variously interpreted by folk etymologists as meaning "producing clouds," "producing seaweed," and "abundant seaweed."

I have mentioned that the waka consists of thirty-one syllables arranged in a certain pattern of lines. Syllabic meters are by no means unknown in the European poetry of the past, and in modern poetry they are perhaps more common than meters based on stress accents, but a mere count of syllables does not, in English at least, provide sufficient rhythmic interest. The stress accent, an integral part of the English language, will be heard, whether or not the poet observes a fixed pattern of stresses such as iambs or dactyls. The modern poet writing in English utilizes these stresses and otherwise enhances his syllabics with forceful syntax. Most earlier poetry in English depended for effectiveness on patterns of stresses or on rhyme. Greek and Latin poetry depended on the length or shortness of vowels to create similar patterns.

The Japanese language lacks a stress accent; in this respect it is rather like French, where the uniform stress on the last syllable of each word makes it impossible for poets to observe the kinds of metrical patterns favored since the Greeks. But whereas French poets, up until the twentieth century at least, regularly employed rhyme, this too was not feasible for Japanese poets—not because rhyme was difficult, but because it was too easy. Japanese words, with the exception of some importations from China, all end in one of five open vowels. The mathematical likelihood of rhyming, whether one wishes to or not, is thus twenty percent. In the poem about the eightfold Izumo fence, for example, the second and third lines rhyme (*yaegaki* and *ni*), as do the first and fourth (*tatsu* and *tsukuru*), but surely this was unintentional. Rhyme is of interest only if it is difficult; if it occurs inevitably, it does not serve to distinguish poetry from prose. The third European metrical scheme, based on quantity, was impossible in classical Japanese because all syllables were of equal weight. It might be possible in modern Japanese, which has both long and short vowels, but as far as I know, no Japanese poet has ever exploited this possibility.

The Japanese were left, then, with syllabics, and this remained true of every variety of Japanese poetry from the eighth to the twentieth century. Under European influence some Japanese wrote rhymed poetry in this manner:

> *haru wa monogoto yorokobashi*
> *fuku kaze totemo atatakashi*
> *niwa no sakura ya momo no hana*
> *yo ni utsukushiku miyuru kana*
> *nobe no hikari wa ito tataku*
> *kumoi haruka ni maite naku*

> In spring everything is full of charm,
> The blowing wind is really warm.
> Cherry and peach, blossoming bright,
> Make an unusually pretty sight.
> The lark of the moors, very high,
> Sings as it soars far in the sky.[2]

2. Translated in Donald Keene, *Landscapes and Portraits: Appreciations of Japanese Culture* (Tokyo: Kodansha International, 1971), p. 135.

This effort by a Japanese poet of the 1870s attempts to get around the inevitability of rhyme by having the last two syllables of each line rhyme, which is somewhat less predictable. Instead of giving the rhyme greater richness, however, the effect is comic, recalling the rhymes in a Gilbert and Sullivan operetta, such as the song in *The Pirates of Penzance* that begins:

> I am the very model of a modern Major General
> I've information vegetable, animal and mineral;
> I know the Kings of England, and I quote the facts historical,
> From Marathon to Waterloo, in order categorical.

Like the poets writing English syllabics today, the poets of the *Man'yōshū*, the great collection compiled about 770, used tightly controlled syntax to overcome the lack of contour that is the problem of such poetry, especially when it is long. Although it is not always apparent in translation, some of the poems of the master poet Kakinomoto no Hitomaro (who died about 715) are syntactically a single sentence. Even in translation his poems are effective, though nothing is conveyed of their metrical or syntactical features. This poem was written after the death of Hitomaro's wife:

> Since in Karu lived my wife,
> I wished to be with her to my heart's content;
> But I could not visit her constantly
> Because of the many watching eyes—
> Men would know of our troth,
> Had I sought her too often.
> So our love remained secret like a rock-pent pool;
> I cherished her in my heart,
> Looking to after-time when we should be together,
> And lived secure in my trust

As one riding a great ship.
Suddenly there came a messenger
Who told me she was dead—
Was gone like a yellow leaf of autumn.
Dead as the day dies with the setting sun,
Lost as the bright moon is lost behind the cloud,
Alas, she is no more, whose soul
Was bent to mine like the bending seaweed!

When the word was brought to me
I knew not what to do nor what to say;
But restless at the mere news,
And hoping to heal my grief
Even a thousandth part,
I journeyed to Karu and searched the market-place
Where my wife was wont to go!

There I stood and listened.
But no voice of her I heard,
Though the birds sang in the Unebi Mountain;
None passed by who even looked like my wife.
I could only call her name and wave my sleeve.[3]

This poem is written throughout in alternating lines of five and seven syllables, with an extra line in seven syllables at the end. It is certainly not unusually long by European standards, but Japanese poets between the eighth and nineteenth centuries found it so difficult to write *chōka* (long poems) that there are few examples, and most of those are tedious. The problem in writing such poetry is that as soon

3. Kakinomoto no Hitomaro, "After the Death of His Wife," in *The Manyōshū*, Nippon Gakujutsu Shinkōkai translation (New York: Columbia University Press, 1965), pp. 42–43. Subsequent quotations from *The Manyōshū* are from this edition.

as the tension in a long poem drops, it becomes not inferior poetry, but prose. There are many lines in the *Iliad* that are merely formulaic, or that are transitions enabling the poet to get from one situation to the next; how often, for example, one encounters lines such as "thus spake unto him godlike Achilles, saying. . . . "If there had been no quantity in Homer's lines, the *Iliad* would have become as tedious in spots as it is in the English prose translations. It is hard also to imagine the strain it would have been on Milton—and on his readers—if he had felt obliged to keep at white-hot intensity every line in *Paradise Lost* for fear it might drop otherwise into prose; fortunately, blank verse kept the poem going even at its prosiest. But the Japanese language did not permit the use of the rhythms of hexameters or pentameters. The alternating lines of five and seven syllables were essential to the poetic forms, but they did not ensure that a composition in such lines would be poetry; there are long passages in novels—which no one has ever thought of as poetry—that are equally in alternating fives and sevens. Unless the content is kept at a distinctively poetic level, a Japanese long poem ceases to be a poem.

Faced with the difficulties of writing long poems in syllabics, the Japanese had another choice, and they took it, though it was one that would have chilled most European poets: it was simply not to write long poems, but to confine themselves to short forms, especially to the waka. During the century before the compilation of the *Man'yōshū*, the need for long poems was closely related to the functions of the poets laureate. Many of Hitomaro's best poems were eulogies for some deceased member of the imperial family, written in his capacity as poet laureate; but with the change in burial customs such eulogies were no longer needed. Under Buddhist influence cremation became normal, and the period between death and cremation was short. This was in contrast to the former practice of keeping the body of a deceased prince or princess in a special mortuary chamber for months at a time where poems of mourning could be addressed to it, assuring the mourned person that he or she would never be forgotten.

Another function of poets laureate of the eighth century was to accompany the sovereign on excursions to different parts of the country and to compose poetry celebrating both the landscapes along the way and the glory of the emperor's or the empress' reign. Yamabe no Akahito, traditionally rated next in greatness to Hitomaro among the *Man'yōshū* poets, composed this poem about 725 to commemorate the visit of the emperor to Yoshino, a place in the mountains southwest of the capital where the imperial family maintained a residence:

> Here in a beautiful dell where the river runs,
> The Yoshino Palace, the high abode
> Of our Sovereign reigning in peace,
> Stands engirdled, fold on fold,
> By green mountain walls.
> In spring the flowers bend the boughs;
> With autumn's coming the mist rises and floats over all.
> Ever prosperous like those mountains
> And continuously as this river flows,
> Will the lords and ladies of the court
> Come hither. (*The Manyōshū*, p. 192)

This is accomplished writing, but it is also rather conventional, even for the time; the contrast made here between spring and autumn does not surprise, as it would if Hitomaro had chosen this subject. But in the fashion of the *Man'yō-shū* poets, Akahito appended two envoys, waka that epitomize the preceding chōka. Here is the second:

nubatama no
yo no fukeyukeba
hisagi ouru
kiyoki kawara ni
chidori shiba naku.

Now the jet-black night deepens:
And on the beautiful river beach,
Where grow the *hisagi* trees,
The sanderlings cry ceaselessly.

This waka seems to me quite perfect. It says more in fewer lines than the chōka that it follows. No doubt this was why poets turned to the waka when the court no longer required poems to commemorate imperial travels or to mourn the deaths of members of the sovereign's family. Of course, many things could not be stated in the thirty-one syllables of a waka, no matter how skillfully composed: a narrative (there are some narrative chōka in the *Man'yōshū*) cannot be related with such brevity; intellectual matters in which the mind as well as the heart is involved can seldom be treated adequately; events of national importance, such as the discovery of gold or the departure of an expedition to subdue unruly elements on the frontier, or the poet's reactions to some social or religious issue, are almost impossible to squeeze into a waka.

Japanese poets sacrificed many of the uses of poetry when they settled on the waka as their almost exclusive poetic form, but they could if they chose have recourse to writing poetry in Chinese, rather as poets in Europe until the nineteenth century wrote sometimes in Latin. The concision of classical Chinese, which all educated men and some women learned, made it possible to express a great deal more in a quatrain than in the five lines of a waka. Moreover, the poets were not obliged to confine themselves to quatrains but, if their skill in handling the Chinese language was up to it, they could write Chinese poems of fifty or even a hundred lines. The Chinese poem was the form of expression utilized by poets when the waka seemed too frail to bear the burden of what they intended to write.

During the ninth century the prestige of Chinese learning was such that at times it must have seemed likely that the Japanese language would be no more than a medium in which to buy groceries or give orders to the servants—a "language of the bazaar," as the modern Indian and Iranian languages used to be called patronizingly by scholars of Sanskrit and Old Persian. Perhaps the chief reason why the waka—and literature in Japanese in general—survived was because old-fashioned ideas concerning education for women persuaded parents that it would be unladylike for their daughters to learn Chinese. (There were exceptions, notably Murasaki Shikibu, the author of *The Tale of Genji*.) This meant that when men addressed poems to women, they had to compose them in Japanese.

The use of poetry as a go-between in courtship was listed in the preface to the first imperially sponsored anthology of Japanese poetry, the *Kokinshū* (905), as one of its principal functions. Unlike Chinese poems, for example, a very large proportion of the waka composed for a thousand years were love poems, even when the ostensible theme was the changing glories of the seasons. Men and women exchanged poetry, both in writing and—as we know from *The Tale of Genji*—orally. The use of poetry for courtship encouraged the development of a distinctive, extremely beautiful calligraphy. Paper appropriate to the content of the poem and ink of appropriate blackness were also important, and when the note (often no more than a single waka) was sent, seasonal flowers might be attached, and—needless to say—an appropriately attired, elegant messenger was also essential. From this time on, the intimate connection between poetry and other arts was established. Paintings were inscribed with suitable poems—but not only paintings. Magnificent kimonos had poems embroidered on them, the lines sometimes scattered over a wide surface, and lacquerwork was similarly decorated. The displacement of the chōka by the waka may have been influenced by the difficulty inherent in the use of the longer form, but the result was fortunate as far as the development of poetry was concerned.

The shorter form lent itself to the billet doux, to extemporaneous responses to some sight of nature, to the fusion of poetry and the visual arts. The Japanese by their own choice forfeited many of the potential uses of poetry, preferring to suggest in a few words a remembered love or the poignance of a hoped-for love, rather than to let forth a full-throated cry of despair over some tragedy to themselves or their country; but what they achieved was often close to perfection, and when the poems were combined with the works of art they inspired, readers were moved by the calligraphy almost as much as by the words.

The waka of the *Kokinshū* were written in *kana*, the script that took the place of the cumbersome system of writing used in the *Man'yōshū*. We do not know who invented the kana, nor even the date, but presumably it was invented in the late eighth or early ninth century by Buddhist priests with some knowledge of Sanskrit. Although the shapes of the kana symbols were derived from Chinese writing, the use of a syllabary—something like an alphabet—quite likely came from India. The word *kana* (originally *kari-na*) meant "temporary names," and was used in contrast with *mana*, "real names" or Chinese characters—the implication being that the kana were no more than temporary substitutes for real writing. The invention of a distinctively Japanese script was part of a general shift that occurred during a period ranging from the ninth to thirteenth centuries, in which various peoples of Eastern Asia turned from an unconditional emulation of China to an assertion of the importance of their own languages and cultures. The Japanese seem to have been the earliest of these peoples to evolve a distinctive writing system.

The ninth century is sometimes called the "dark age" of Japanese poetry. The prestige of Chinese civilization was so high that poets at the court scorned to write Japanese. It was thanks to women (and to the men who addressed poems to women) that the waka survived. The most celebrated of the ninth-century women poets, Ono no Komachi, became a legend in her own time or shortly thereafter: she is said to have been a peerless beauty, desired by all men at the court, but also a cruel woman who subjected her would-be lovers to extreme unkindness. Another group of legends refers to Komachi in old age, when she wandered in rags, her beauty gone and her appearance so wretched that she was mocked wherever she went. Finally, there are stories of Komachi's death and of her skull lying in a field, where the wind, blowing through the holes that were her eyes, made a mournful sound that told of her anguish.

The surviving poems of Komachi are almost all in a melancholy vein, typified by her best-known waka:

> *hana no iro wa*
> *utsurinikeri na*
> *itazura ni*
> *wa ga mi yo ni furu*
> *nagame seshi ma ni*

The flowers withered,
Their color faded away.

While meaninglessly
I spent my days in brooding
And the long rains were falling.[4]

The poem has been interpreted as referring solely to the speaker: the colors of my springtime (that is, my beauty) faded while meaninglessly I spent my time in affairs with men and brooded over my fate. It can also be interpreted as a description of the passage of the spring: the color of the cherry blossoms faded to no purpose while the long rains were falling. Two such interpretations are possible because some words have double meanings. *Furu*, a form of the verb *fu*, means "to spend time," but it is a homonym both of *furu*, meaning "to fall" (of rain), and of *furu*, "to become old." Again, *nagame* is not only *naga-ame*, or "long rain," but part of the verb *nagamu*, meaning "to stare at" or "to brood." The use of such verbal dexterity enabled poets to say a great deal more in thirty-one syllables than one might expect, but the expression is sometimes so elliptical that there have been many disputes about the precise meaning of the poem.

The *Kokinshū* of 905 was compiled by court officials who were charged with assembling a collection that would meet with the emperor's approval and add to the glory of his reign. Most of the poems were composed by members of the lower ranks of the aristocracy. The reluctance of the great nobles to contribute was probably not a sign of poetic incompetence, but of lingering reluctance to compose poetry in Japanese. No poets of the *Kokinshū* are identified as being commoners, though some anonymous poems may have been written away from the court. At the time literacy was confined largely to the aristocracy and the priesthood, and it is

4. My translation, in Donald Keene, *Landscapes and Portraits: Appreciations of Japanese Culture* (Tokyo: Kodansha International, 1971), p. 31.

therefore not surprising that contributors to a court anthology should have been restricted, but the *Kokinshū* created an aristocratic tradition in Japanese literature that contrasts with the plebeian traditions of, say, English literature.

The chief compiler of the *Kokinshū*, Ki no Tsurayuki, wrote a preface to the collection that is a first statement of the ideals of Japanese poetry. He listed, for example, the circumstances under which the poets he admired had composed waka:

> . . . when they saw the blossoms fall on a spring morning, or heard the leaves fall of an autumn evening; or when they sighed to see the drifts of snow and ripples reflected in their mirrors increase with each passing year; or when they were startled into realizing the brevity of life on noticing dew on the grass or foam on the water; or when, having fallen in the world, they have become estranged from those they loved.

These occasions for writing poetry can be resumed under a single general theme, regret over the changes brought about by the passage of time, which is indeed a dominant theme of the collection, and perhaps the quality that distinguished the *Kokinshū* most conspicuously from the Chinese anthologies of poetry that were most admired by the Japanese. Nostalgia for the past is a key to the understanding of Japanese poetry. This was true even when the Japanese composed poetry in Chinese: the first collection of such poems, compiled in 751, was called *Kaifūsō*, "Fond Recollections of Poetry."

Seasonal poems make up the first six of the twenty books of the *Kokinshū*. Two books each were devoted to spring and autumn poetry, and one each to summer and winter. A very large proportion of the waka composed for the next thousand years would describe the seasons, either directly or as revealed by characteristic phenomena such as mist, haze, fog, and so on. In time some seasonal words became arbitrary: for example, the moon, unless qualified by another seasonal word, was always the moon in autumn, when its light was most appreciated. In the haiku, a poetic genre not invented until the sixteenth century, the presence of a seasonal word was not merely desirable but absolutely essential. Japanese today often explain this absorption with the seasons in terms of the distinctiveness of each of the four seasons in Japan, but it would be hard to prove that the four seasons are more conspicuously distinguished there than in any other country. Suffice it to say that Japanese poets have been unusually sensitive to the changes that accompany the seasons.

Summer and winter poems, as I have said, were accorded only half the space given to spring and autumn poems. This preference among the seasons may reflect the climate of Kyoto, where spring and autumn are delectable but the summers stifling and the winters bitter cold. The choice of the flowers and birds celebrated in the *Kokinshū* was probably also influenced by what the poets admired in Kyoto. In the *Man'yōshū*, the flowers celebrated most often are plum blossoms, as in China; but when the the capital was moved late in the eighth century from Nara, famous for its plum blossoms, to Kyoto, cherry blossoms, the typical flowers of Kyoto, were described instead—so often in waka poetry that one modern critic has written that if one were compelled to read all the poems on cherry blossoms in the imperial collections, one would end up by detesting them. Similarly, the *hototogisu*, a bird that was common in Kyoto, appears very frequently in *Kokinshū* poetry. The preferences of the capital always tended to spread to other parts of the country, and even poets who lived in places where a hototogisu was never heard dutifully mentioned this bird in their summer poems.

Ki no Tsurayuki's preface to the *Kokinshū* claimed that "poetry, without effort, moves heaven and earth, stirs the feelings of the invisible gods and spirits, smooths the relations of men and women, and calms the hearts of fierce warriors." The only one of these characteristics that bears direct relation to the contents of the *Kokinshū* is poetry's capacity to smooth the relations between men and women. Love poetry is certainly conspicuous in the *Kokinshū*, following the tradition of the age of Komachi, when almost *all* poetry was love poetry. The insistence of the preface on the importance of love and other emotions was not a truism: miracles of the gods, battles fought by heroes, moral principles, and other nonemotional subjects could have inspired great poetry in Japan as elsewhere in the world, but the Japanese seem to have felt that writing about such subjects was not a legitimate function of waka poetry.

Although Japanese poetry was credited with the power to move gods and demons, its themes tended to be subdued. Tsurayuki reported of the Japanese poets of the past that "they admired flowers, envied birds their song, were moved by the mists, and stirred by the dew." Such themes were well suited to court poets for whom blunt, straightforward expressions of feeling would have seemed crude. These poets sought perfection in their language, in the order of their words and the music of the successive syllables, even more than in the surface meanings of their poems. Not infrequently poets borrowed from their predecessors, using the imagery or the overall conception of an older poem but changing the emphasis or wording. This was not plagiarism, but perfectionism; it was assumed that the source poem would be recognized and that the skill with which the new suggestion of the happiness of love; the poets wrote most often about the unresponsiveness of the beloved, the failure of the beloved to pay a promised visit, even the acceptance of death as the only resolution of an unhappy affair, as if joy were unseemly.

The images in the *Kokinshū* poetry tend to be repeated. Many poems describe cherry blossoms, but none the beauty of peach blossoms. Even if a court poet happened to have been moved by peach blossoms, he probably would not have wished to be so eccentric as to describe them rather than such accepted themes as the scent of plum blossoms or the white clouds of cherry blossoms. Unusual imagery or subjects tended to attract attention to themselves, and the poets preferred imagery that was transparent because of its very familiarity, permitting readers to see through the words of the poem to the emotion being evoked. The poems chosen for inclusion in the *Kokinshū* reflect the preferences of the editors, and poems with unusual imagery or language were rejected, though sometimes retrieved by the compilers of later anthologies. It is clear, in any case, that by their choices of poems the compilers established a poetic diction—some two thousand words in all—that with only minor additions would be employed by the waka poets of the next thousand years. Not only was the vocabulary restricted, but the associations of the various flowers, trees, and birds were forever established. The prestige of the poetic diction of the *Kokinshū* was so great that later poets who lived in quite different times were obliged to restrict themselves to a vocabulary that was incapable of describing contemporary life. One might imagine that poets of the eighteenth century would have fretted over the restrictions imposed on their expression by an arbitrarily established poetic diction, but they not only worshipped the *Kokinshū* but seem not to have wanted poet altered the old poem to suit his individual tastes or the tastes of a different age would be appreciated. Many subjects could not be treated at all, however, because they were considered to be vulgar, or at any rate unattractive. This attitude perhaps prevented the court poets from describing large areas of human experience, but they did not feel frustrated.

The conventions of life at the court favored artificiality and even insincerity in poetic composition. Poets were expected to compose verse on prescribed topics, whether or not of interest or personal relevance. A love poem by the priest Sosei illustrates the point:

> ima kon to
> iishi bakari ni
> nagatsuki no
> ariake no tsuki o
> machiidetsuru kana

> by and by I'll come
> he said and so I waited
> patiently but I
> saw only the moon of the
> longest month in the dawn sky[5]

Not only was it inappropriate for a Buddhist priest to write a love poem, but this one was written using the persona of a woman. Little of the love poetry in the *Kokinshū* is sincere, in the way that the poems of Komachi strike us as being sincere. The craftsmanship is admirable, but one does not often hear distinctive voices, and the mood is more often bittersweet than either tragic or joyous. Rarely is there a

5. Sosei, in *Kokinshū*, Laurel Rasplica Rodd, trans., with Mary Catherine Henkenius (Princeton, N.J.: Princeton University Press, 1984), p. 248.

to venture beyond its themes. Cherry blossoms were as lovely in the eighteenth century as in the tenth, and their blossoming or falling excited similar reactions, even if the poet was a merchant, a class of people the compiler Tsura-yuki would not have believed capable of poetic utterance. If a merchant-poet wished to describe his daily life he would have had to violate the established poetic diction, which lacked words for the food he ate, the clothes he wore, the tobacco he smoked, the business in which he was engaged, the licensed quarter of prostitution that he frequented. Of course, if a merchant-poet really found the *Kokinshū* vocabulary confining, he could write in some new genre such as haiku, which was free of such restrictions of language.

The *Kokinshū* style was created for a relatively small number of people, the members of the Japanese court at a particularly brilliant period. The courtiers, unlike their equivalents in Europe, had little or no interest in hunting and were never called upon to participate in a war. Their days were taken up with matters of ceremony, precedence, and decorum that are of no interest today. They are remembered almost exclusively for the poetry they wrote. They passed on to future generations—the whole Japanese people and not only aristocrats—an aesthetic appreciation of the world that is not found elsewhere. The *Kokinshū* poets demonstrated the Japanese ability to empathize with nature, to find significance in the fall of a leaf or in a gesture, and to capture instants of aesthetic awareness in poetry of exquisite melody.

Perhaps the most beautiful statement ever made about Japanese poetry occurs in the Nō play *Sekidera Komachi:*

The words of poetry will never fail.
They are enduring as evergreen boughs of pine,

Continuous as trailing branches of willow;
For poetry, whose source and seed is found
In the human heart, is everlasting.
Though ages pass and all things vanish,
Poems will leave their marks behind,
And the traces of poetry will never disappear.[6]

6. Translated by Karen Brazell, in Donald Keene, ed., *Twenty Plays of the Nō Theatre* (New York: Columbia University Press, 1970), p. 71.

THREE

THE USES OF JAPANESE POETRY

TO GIVE A chapter the title "The Uses of Japanese Poetry" may seem rather paradoxical; to poets, it may even seem a profanation. A contemporary poet, if asked the *use* of his poetry, would assume that the question was unfriendly, that the questioner was implying that unlike other arts—such as painting, which is useful in hiding blank spaces on walls, or music, useful in inducing factory workers to perform their tasks more cheerfully—poetry serves no practical purpose. That is not my intent, but I do think it important to note that for long periods poetry was considered to be very useful. Some examples of useful poems in English will suggest what I mean: "Early to bed and early to rise,/ Makes a man healthy, wealthy and wise." Regardless of whether the sentiment expressed in these lines of poetry is true, it is clear that their purpose was not to express the poet's perceptions of beauty, but to communicate a useful bit of information. This example of homespun truth comes from *Poor Richard's Almanac* by Benjamin Franklin. Not all maxims are in verse, of course, but the rhyme makes the wisdom purveyed seem immutable, and the rhythm makes the lesson easier to remember.

Another useful verse will make the point even clearer:

> Thirty days hath November,
> April, June, and September.
> February hath twenty-eight alone,
> And all the rest have thirty-one.

Everybody is familiar with at least the first two lines of this poem by Richard Grafton, a sixteenth-century printer whose poetry is otherwise largely forgotten. The last two lines are harder to remember because of the limping metrics and faulty rhyme, and attempts have been made to improve them; but the essential information—which months have thirty days and which have thirty-one—is perfectly conveyed by the poem. I still have occasion to murmur the poem to myself when in doubt about the length of a particular month. The poem, at least for me, definitely has its use.

Edmund Wilson's collection *The Triple Thinkers* (1938) contains the essay "Is Verse a Dying Technique?" In it Wilson stated: "The important thing to recognize is that the technique of verse was once commonly used for many purposes for which we now ordinarily use prose. Solon expressed his political ideas in verse; the 'Works and Days' is a shepherd's calendar in verse; the 'Theogony' is versified mythology; and almost everything which in contemporary writing would be put into prose plays and novels was versified by the Greeks in epics or plays."

Wilson noted, however, that as far back as Aristotle it was recognized that meter alone was not enough to make a work a poem. Aristotle wrote in the *Poetics* that even if a theory of medicine or physical philosophy was presented in a metrical form, it was unusual to describe the writer as a poet rather than as a doctor or philosopher. Not only the Greeks but the Romans wrote treatises in verse, on philosophy, astronomy, and farming. Lucretius' *De Rerum Natura* has often been admired for its poetry, but it was primarily intended to be useful, not to give aesthetic pleasure. Innumerable other examples might be given, even from fairly recent times, of poetry being used for purposes that are now satisfied by prose. In the nineteenth century novels in verse such as *Aurora Leigh* and *The Ring and the Book* were not only admired but read, though Coleridge had already denied that every excellent work in meter should be considered a poem. He defined a poem in these terms: "A poem is that species of composition which is opposed to works of science by proposing for its immediate object pleasure, not truth; and from all other species . . . it is discriminated by proposing to itself such delight from the *whole* as is compatible with a distinct gratification from each component part." Later critics in Europe and America further refined Coleridge's definitions, until only what we might call "pure poetry"—that is, poetry that has no other use but to give pleasure at some level—was recognized as poetry. T. S. Eliot declared that "for us, anything that can be said as well in prose can be said better in prose."

Eliot declined to define what a poem is, but he suggested that "poetry begins . . . with a savage beating a drum in a jungle, and it retains that essential of percussion and rhythm." And, this most learned of poets declared, "I myself should like an audience which could neither read nor write."

This long prologue has brought me at last to Japanese poetry. Japanese poetry begins not with a savage beating a drum in a jungle, but with some very primitive utterances:

LEFT: Achime!
        Oh, oh, oh, oh!
RIGHT: *Oke*
        Achime!
        Oh, oh, oh, oh!
LEFT: *Oke.*
BOTH: Oh, oh, oh!
RIGHT: *Oke.*[1]

In chapter 2 I mentioned the oldest surviving Japanese book, the *Kojiki* or "Record of Ancient Matters," presented to the court in 712, which contains many poems. Some are only slightly more evolved than the Achime song, but greater attention to form and meaning can be detected even in poems that are said to be utterances of the gods. Here is one:

> Then O-mae-wo-mae-no sukune, lifting up his arms and hitting his thighs, came out dancing and singing. His song said:
>
> > Because the little bell
> > On the garter of the noble
> > Has fallen off,
> > The nobles are all astir.
> > You commoners also, take care![2]

Unlike the pure incantation of the Achime song, this one has a meaning, but precisely what meaning is not clear. Probably people of the time knew more of the background than is recorded in the *Kojiki,* and singing and acting might

1. Translated by Konishi Jin'ichi, in *A History of Japanese Literature* (Princeton, N.J.: Princeton University Press, 1984–), vol. 1, p. 87.
2. *Kojiki,* Donald L. Phillipi, trans. (Tokyo: University of Tokyo Press, 1968), p. 335. Subsequent quotations from the *Kojiki* are from this edition.

have imparted additional sense. One commentator has interpreted the poem as meaning, "A nobleman has seduced a
commoner woman—therefore, commoners, take care!" If
that is so, we have an early instance of a poem having been
used for a worldly purpose. Toward the end of the same
section of the *Kojiki*, Prince Karu sings this song to his
beloved:

> On the river of Hatsuse
> > Of the hidden country,
> In the upper shallows
> > A sacred post was staked,
> In the lower shallows
> > A true post was staked.
> On the sacred post
> > Was hung a mirror,
> On the true post
> > Was hung a jewel.
> My beloved,
> > Who is to me as a mirror,
> My spouse,
> > Who is to me as a jewel—
> Only if I hear
> > That she is there,
> Do I wish to go home,
> > Do I yearn for my country.

Thus singing, they committed suicide together.

Conscious literary intent can be detected in this poem,
especially in the parallelism. The use of the *makurakotoba*
(fixed epithet) "of the hidden country" for Hatsuse, and of
the honorific prefixes *i* (sacred) and *ma* (true) to give greater
dignity to the posts, would also recur in later poetry. But
still one may ask, how can we be sure this is a poem? It is

metrically irregular, the lines varying from three to eight syllables; and there is neither rhyme nor an obvious rhythmic pattern. Moreover, it is not clear why the sacred posts are mentioned, nor why the speaker is so uncertain about the whereabouts of his beloved if he is in fact singing the poem to her. In other words, we do not know the use of the poem. We can guess that it had religious significance. The sacred post, hung with mirrors and jewels, was probably used during a rite. But what kind of rite? And why was this poem needed? One eminent scholar has suggested that the poem was an elegy, and when it states, "Only if I hear that she is there,/ Do I wish to go home,/ Do I yearn for my country" we are meant to understand that she is not there because she is dead, and that he has no desire to go home. But that does not explain the sacred post. Perhaps that is why other scholars have interpreted the poem as a dirge that was originally a prayer for a safe journey; but such a complicated interpretation suggests that these scholars are desperate.

Of one thing we can be sure. The compilers of the *Kojiki* considered the poem so important that it had to be preserved in its exact wording. The parts of the *Kojiki* in prose were written in Chinese characters, used for their meanings. A Chinese, even if he knew no Japanese, could understand these parts, though the wording is sometimes barbarous. But the poems were recorded with Chinese characters used for their sounds, without consideration of the meanings. The compilers used this cumbersome method of transcribing the sounds of Japanese—one character for each syllable of a long word—because the sounds themselves had value, a kind of magic that went beyond the mere meaning. When stories were told about the mythological past of the Japanese, the teller, following the prose framework given in the *Kojiki*, may have extemporized the Japanese words he used;

but the poems, as the sacred utterances of gods and human beings who were close to gods, had to be quoted exactly, even if the meanings were not understood. The purpose of the *Kojiki* poetry was to transmit essential truths in a form that could be memorized with relative ease.

About fifty years after the compilation of the *Kojiki* the greatest collection of Japanese poetry, the *Man'yōshū*, was put into more or less its present shape. It is almost inconceivable that Japanese poetry could have evolved so rapidly. Many poems in the *Man'yōshū* were in fact composed well before the presentation of the *Kojiki* in 712. Of course the songs in the *Kojiki* represent the state of Japanese poetry not at the time of the compilation, but much earlier; but the contrast between the primitive *Kojiki* poetry and the supremely accomplished *Man'yōshū* poetry is overwhelming.

The poems of the *Man'yōshū* can be divided into public and private poems. The uses of the public poems especially have been the focus of critical researches over the years. The most conspicuous feature of these poems in terms of their form is that many are chōka, poems ranging in length up to a hundred and fifty lines—though the five-line waka, the predominant form employed in the *Man'yōshū*, would soon become virtually the only Japanese poetic form. The chief use of the chōka, as we have seen, was probably in eulogizing the recently deceased. In addition to accompanying the sovereign on pleasure excursions and commemorating them, it was the task of court poets to write laments for the deceased members of the imperial family, usually during the period when they were lying in state at a temporary shrine (*arakinomiya*) prior to interment. It was believed that such poems of mourning would comfort the dead and keep them from returning to this world, dissatisfied by the neglect of the living, to torment people.

The eulogy Kakinomoto no Hitomaro wrote for Prince

Takechi opens with a panegyric of the prince's father, then describes how the father, the Emperor Temmu, commanded Takechi to subjugate the enemies of the court. At this juncture,

> Forthwith our prince buckled on a sword,
> And in his august hand
> Grasped a bow to lead the army.
> The drums marshalling men in battle array
> Sounded like the rumbling thunder,
> The war-horns blew, as tigers roar,
> Confronting an enemy,
> Till banners hoisted aloft swayed
> As sway in the wind the flames that burn
> On every moorland far and near
> When spring comes after winter's prisonment.[3]

The poem goes on to describe the prince's mighty deeds. Hitomaro was probably too young to have witnessed the warfare he described so vividly. Scholars have pointed out that the language he employed was strikingly similar to that used in the *Nihon Shoki* (Chronicles of Japan) in describing the same battle, and that account in turn was borrowed from passages in the Chinese dynastic history of the Latter Han. This does not mean that Hitomaro merely translated into Japanese an existing Chinese text; what he reports is essentially true, but the existence of a Chinese model helped him to move beyond the incoherent, poorly organized descriptions of events that typified previous Japanese poetry.

The final section of the eulogy for Prince Takechi describes the palace he built. The poet asks rhetorically if this

3. Kakinomoto no Hitomaro, in *The Manyōshū*, Nippon Gakujutsu Shinkōkai translation (New York: Columbia University Press, 1965), p. 39. Subsequent quotations from *The Manyōshū* are from this edition.

palace, built to last "ten thousand generations," will ever disappear; he implies that even though Prince Takechi is no more, his works will last forever. By reassuring the dead person in this manner, the poet sought to calm his soul (*chinkon*) and assure him that it was unnecessary to return to the world as an angry ghost. To stress the permanence of worldly achievements was by no means typical of the Japanese. The Buddhist conviction that the present world is transitory, even a deceit, was shared by Hitomaro and by most other *Man'yōshū* poets, who often lamented the impermanence of even the most splendid works of man. But in his capacity as a court poet, Hitomaro had no choice but to celebrate not only the prince's appearance and his behavior, but his achievements.

In other eulogies Hitomaro related with conviction the grief of a prince or princess after the death of a wife or husband, mentioning even details of their bedchamber he could not have known, as in this poem presented to Princess Hatsusebe after the death of her husband:

> Dainty water-weeds, growing up-stream
> In the river of the bird-flying Asuka,
> Drift down-stream, gracefully swaying.
> Like the water-weeds the two would bend
> Each towards the other, the princess and her consort.

> But now no longer can she sleep,
> With his fine smooth body clinging
> Close to hers like a guardian sword.
> Desolate must be her couch at night.
> (*The Manyōshū*, p. 36)

Writing about people he did not know might have resulted in the hackneyed sentiments commonly voiced by poets laureate when obliged to produce poems on matters that do not involve them personally, but Hitomaro seems not to have felt such sharp differences between the public and the private, the individual and the group, as later poets would feel; and the exactness of his images when describing the grief of a princess makes us feel, against reason perhaps, that he somehow shared her sorrow. Ironically, Hitomaro is so convincing in his poems on subjects that he could not have known from personal experience that doubts have been expressed about the truthfulness of poems that describe his own emotions; it has been argued that if he could so persuasively describe the sadness of some inaccessible princess, there is no reason why he could not also have invented a persona for himself and written in the manner he imagined a poet would write, say, when his wife died. But reading Hitomaro's two great poems on the death of his wife—one of them is quoted on pp. 29–30, in chapter 2—it is difficult to question their authenticity.

Hitomaro wrote a number of poems celebrating the travels to Yoshino and other places by the Empress Jitō, who came to the throne in 686 after the death of her husband Temmu and ruled until her death in 702. Hitomaro's devotion to Jitō and the imperial family was absolute; it cannot be doubted that he believed that the empress he served was a goddess:

> Our great Sovereign, a goddess,
> Of her sacred will
> Has reared a towering palace
> On Yoshino's shore,
> Encircled by its rapids;
> And, climbing, she surveys the land.
> The overlapping mountains,
> Rising like green walls,

Offer their blossoms with spring,
As godly tributes to the Throne.
The god of the Yū River, to provide the royal table
Holds the cormorant-fishing
In its upper shallows,
And sinks the fishing-nets
In the lower stream.
Thus the mountains and the river
Serve our Sovereign, one in will;
It is truly the reign of a divinity.
                                        (*The Manyōshū*, p. 29)

In this poem Hitomaro not only expresses his belief in the divinity of the Empress Jitō but declares that the gods of the mountains and rivers pay her homage. Jitō's act of survey-ing the land *(kunimi)* had special significance if one believed with the poet that a blood relationship existed between the sovereign and the land she ruled.

Another use of poetry, found uniquely in the *Man'yōshū* among all the old anthologies of Japanese poetry, is the social criticism of Yamanoue no Okura. Okura's reputation has sharply risen during the twentieth century, until he is now ranked second only to Hitomaro among the *Man'yōshū* poets. This revaluation has been occasioned by modern ap-preciation of the special content of his poems. Most Japanese poetry written before the twentieth century is devoid of intellectual or social concern, though it beautifully captures emotional states and the poets' perceptions of nature. Oku-ra's poems are among the rare exceptions. They are some-times introduced by long prefaces that explain not merely the circumstances of composition but the underlying philos-ophy, whether Buddhist, Confucian, or Taoist. Some poems have relatively uncomplicated content, such as one in which Okura declares that nothing is more important than one's children, or another in which he insists that provincial governors must acquaint themselves with local customs. Other poems, though on equally familiar themes such as the impermanence of life and the sufferings that come with old age, are so powerfully expressed that the reader soon forgets whatever similarities exist between Okura's poems and those on similar themes by other poets. His poem on the "difficulties of living in this world" contains this vivid passage:

> Few are the nights they keep,
> When, sliding back the plank doors,
> They reach their beloved ones,
> And sleep, arms intertwined,
> Before, with staffs at their waists,
> They totter along the road,
> Laughed at here, and hated there.
> (*The Manyōshū*, p. 202)

The most famous poem by Okura is his "Dialogue on Poverty," a conversation between two men, the first a poor but proud man who wonders how people worse off than himself manage to survive, the second a destitute man who indirectly responds by describing his misery. The second man's lament begins:

> Wide as they call the heaven and earth,
> For me they have shrunk quite small;
> Bright though they call the sun and moon,
> They never shine for me.
> Is it the same for all men,
> Or for me alone?
> By rare chance I was born a man
> And no meaner than my fellows,
> But wearing unwadded sleeveless clothes
> In tatters, like weeds waving in the sea,

Hanging from my shoulders,
And under the sunken roof,
Within the leaning walls,
Here I lie on straw
Spread on the bare earth,
With my parents at my feet,
All huddled in grief and tears.

(*The Manyōshū*, p. 206)

During the next thousand years no other poem like this would be composed in Japanese. Okura's ability to enter into the feelings of persons of far lower social position may have been fostered by his observations while he served as the governor of a remote province, but it is remarkable all the same that he should have considered two such unpoetical figures as the subjects of his poem. Later poets sought to achieve elegance in their language, but Okura seems to have deliberately avoided all elegance, whether in word or thought, choosing plain and even unpleasant images in order to make his portraits of the two men convincing. His concern for the cold and hungry reflected his Confucian training, and the "use" of this poem was probably to admonish officials who were indifferent to the misery of the common people.

Later poets, even if they were also officials who had passed examinations on the Confucian classics, rarely expressed such views in their waka; but poets who wrote in Chinese often followed Chinese rather than Japanese traditions. The principal use of poetry, as defined long before in China and accepted by many Japanese writers of *kanshi*, poems composed in classical Chinese, was to help promote good government. The largest collection of kanshi of the ninth century was the imperially sponsored collection called *Keikokushū* (Collection of Poems for Governing the Country), and many poems in this collection were written with this aim. The

Confucian justification for the existence of poetry, like the
Buddhist interpretation of all forms of art as a *hōben* (expe-
dient) that helped people to understand difficult religious
doctrine—or Lucretius' characterization of poetry as honey
on the lip of a cup of wormwood which helped a person to
swallow bitter but essential medicine—may not have been
truly accepted even by poets who solemnly insisted that this
was their purpose; but it has always been hard for people to
value things that have no clearly defined use. When a man
wrote poems in Japanese, he normally did not try to assist
in good government or promote the salvation of others; the
uses of the kanshi and the waka remained distinct. That may
be why Okura's "Dialogue on Poverty" exercised no influence on later poetry in Japanese and was not accorded much
special attention until the twentieth century.

The great majority of *Man'yōshū* poems are waka, which
became the classic verse form. Many waka in this collection
that seem to be no more than love songs or impressions of
travel have been interpreted in terms of hidden religious
content. Mention of twilight, for example, or of birds has
been interpreted in terms of the Japanese dread of the twilight hour or of the belief that birds were messengers from
the world of the dead. But the private poems in the *Man'
yōshū* cannot *all* have been intended to convey such meanings; probably, as Chinese thought became generally known
at the court, the original meanings of many terms were
forgotten and they were used as part of a poetic, rather than
religious, tradition.

The most important early statement on the nature of
Japanese court poetry is found in Ki no Tsurayuki's preface
to the *Kokinshū*, the first officially sponsored anthology of
waka poetry, presented to the court in 905. As noted in
chapter 2, in his preface Tsurayuki attributed to poetry the
power to smooth the relations of men and women. Love

poetry was in fact virtually the only kind of poetry written in Japanese during the ninth century, the dark age of the waka, when courtiers who usually expressed their thoughts in Chinese verse wrote waka mainly for presentation to women, who normally did not learn Chinese. Love poetry came to occupy an extremely prominent place in Japanese literature, second only to poetry describing the seasons. In this respect Japanese poetry differs from Chinese poetry, in which few works by the major poets were devoted to love. Poems on friendship, so common in Chinese literature, are virtually nonexistent in Japan, but poems on love were so central an element in the Japanese tradition that even persons for whom the composition of love poetry was inappropriate often wrote poems on topics like parting the morning after a meeting. Writing this kind of poetry demonstrated that a given priest or an aged courtier, whatever the realities of his life, was not insensitive to the most moving of human experiences; and an ability to compose poetry, regardless of the topic, was useful in obtaining recognition and sometimes even advancement at court.

Tsurayuki's preface also mentioned that Japanese poetry has the power to calm the hearts of fierce warriors. In the West soldier-poets are not unknown, but they tend to express themselves in poems addressed to the "Lord God of Battles." The Japanese soldier-poets, even in the thick of battle, wrote of the changing beauties of the seasons. A famous section of The Tale of the Heike relates how Taira no Tadanori (1144–1184), hearing that his teacher of waka poetry Fujiwara Shunzei was about to compile a new court anthology of poetry, risked death by going to the capital, then full of enemy soldiers, to plead with Shunzei to include one of his poems in the new collection. Shunzei eventually complied with the request, though he prudently listed the poem as anonymous so as not to offend Tadanori's enemies,

the new rulers of Japan. Here is the poem for which Tadanori risked his life:

sazanami ya
Shiga no miyako wa
arenishi wo
mukashi nagara no
yamazakura kana

The capital at
Shiga of the little waves
Has fallen to ruins;
But, unchanged from long ago,
The mountain cherry-blossoms.

Perhaps an allegorical meaning was intended: Tadanori
mentioned the ancient capital at Shiga on the shores of Lake
Biwa ("of little waves"), but he may have been thinking of
Kyoto, where the Taira power was now in ruins, though the
cherry trees still bloomed as beautifully as ever. It is not
necessary, however, to search for hidden meanings; an
evocation of the mountain cherry-blossoms amid the ruins
of the old capital at Shiga may have been all that Tadanori
intended. The poem had served its purpose by calming his
warrior's heart at a time of great turbulence.

From this time on there was a tradition of soldiers composing valedictory verses to the world *(jisei)*, in which they
indirectly communicated frustration, regret over the shortness of their lives, joy over having been able to serve the
emperor, or whatever their prevailing sentiment was, usually in terms of cherry blossoms or autumn leaves. Why
should a fierce warrior have chosen to die with a poem on
his lips rather than with some terrible imprecation? To en-
capsulate his thoughts in the shape of a waka lent dignity to
his last moments, associating him with the surrounding

scenery and the Japanese tradition of poetic expression. This use of poetry continued to as recently as 1970, when Mishima Yukio and his disciples in the Shield Society composed farewell poems before they broke into the headquarters of the Eastern Defense Force.

During the Heian period (794–1185), poetry became increasingly involved with the court, as we know from the many *uta-awase,* or poem competitions, held under the sponsorship of the emperor or some other member of the imperial family. Much of this poetry was composed on assigned topics, and the success or failure of a given poem at a competition was judged on the basis of its fulfillment of the specifications of the topic, rather than on its originality or strength of feeling. But although the poetry was composed by members of the court, court business never openly figured in the poems, as it does in the poem by Po Chü-i which ends:

Today when I heard of your appointment as Secretary of the
    Water Board
I was far more pleased than when myself I became secretary to
    a board.[4]

The Japanese poet at most hinted at disappointment over his failure to rise in the hierarchy, as in this poem by Fujiwara no Toshiyori:

> *yo no naka wa*
> *ukimi ni soeru*
> *kage nare ya*
> *omoisutsuredo*
> *hanarezarikeri*

4. Translated by Arthur Waley, in *The Life and Times of Po Chü-i* (New York: Macmillan, 1951), p. 146.

Is this world of ours
A shadow somehow attached
To my luckless self?
Although I try to shake free,
It refuses to leave me.

The brevity of the waka form and the restrictive poetic diction may have inhibited poets who wished to discuss their daily concerns in waka, but most poets probably did not consider their political careers a fit subject for poetry.

The only words of non-Japanese origin that were tolerated in the waka were Buddhist terms. Buddhist poems appeared with increasing frequency in the successive court anthologies, especially as the Heian period drew toward its tragic close. The waka form in such cases was used for the communication of religious rather than emotional perceptions, as in this poem by Toshiyori:

Amida butsu no
tonauru koe wa
kaji nite ya
kurushiki umi wo
kogihanaruran

My voice invoking
The name of Amida Buddha
Shall be my rudder
And I will row away across
The sea of misery.

In the Heian period, poetry was often used to decorate paintings, and the Toshiyori poem above bears the headnote: "Written on a place in a painting that depicts a priest boarding a boat at the West Gate of the Tennōji, where he is rowed westwards away from the shore." The misery of life in this world was often likened to a sea of pain *(kukai)*, and the Buddhist law was compared to a boat that enabled the believer to traverse that sea. Apparently there was also a superstition that if a person left by boat from the West Gate of the Tennōji, the great temple in Ōsaka, then jumped into the sea and drowned, he would go straight to Amida's paradise in the west. It is not clear whether or not Toshiyori had this in mind. Elsewhere he expressed his belief that poetry was of immense help in gaining salvation, an early sounding of the justification for literature that would be common in the medieval period.

The most typical poetic form of the medieval age, especially the fourteenth and fifteenth centuries, was *renga*, or linked verse. Renga was essentially a group activity. Far more than waka competitions, renga sessions brought people together, not to compose rival poems but to join in contributing to the creation of a single work of art. The appeal of renga composition was particularly strong during periods of warfare and other disasters because renga met the need for human companionship. The primary function of renga was to bring people together in the pleasure of artistic composition, sometimes lofty, sometimes comic or even bawdy. But this was not renga's only use. The first power of the waka that Tsurayuki named in his preface to the *Kokinshū* was its ability to move heaven and earth and to stir the feelings of the gods and demons. This use of poetry in medieval Japan was typified by the renga sequences offered to Shintō shrines in the hope that the gods, pleased by the poetry, would vouchsafe favors. In 1471 a *hokku* (opening verse) offered by Sōgi to the Mishima Shrine in Izu was credited with the miraculous cure of a child. In 1504 Sōchō offered at the same shrine a renga sequence in one thousand links with the expectation that it would assure a victory in warfare for the *daimyō* he served.

Another medieval use of poetry was for divination. The

Nō play *Utaura* has for its chief character *(shite)* a male medium who predicts the future from the poem that a client touches out of a group of poem slips. The shite identifies himself as a Shintō priest from a shrine in the province of Ise. A villager, hearing of the priest's reputation as a diviner, comes to ask two questions; he brings with him a child. The man wants to know, first, if his own ailing father will recover from his present illness. He draws a poem, and the priest interprets it as meaning that the father will live out a long life. Next, the villager asks about the child's father, whose whereabouts are unknown. Again he chooses a slip, and finds this poem written on it:

> *uguisu no*
> *kaiko no naka no*
> *hototogisu*
> *sha ga chichi ni nite*
> *sha ga chichi ni nizu*

> From within the egg
> Inside the nightingale's nest
> A cuckoo was born:
> It resembles its father,
> It does not look like its father.

This cryptic poem, which is fairly close to the opening of a *Man'yōshū* chōka, refers to the cuckoo's habit of laying its eggs in another bird's nest. The priest interprets the poem as meaning that the boy has already found his lost father— who is in fact the diviner himself. Divination is possible because the waka itself partakes of the divine.

On another, less elevated level, renga was also used in gambling. After the topic for a renga sequence was set, participants composed verses that were awarded points for excellence. Persons with the highest number of points were

given prizes. Before long people were betting at renga sessions on which poets would carry off the prizes. Renga
sessions came to resemble gambling parties, and at times
they were prohibited by the authorities because of the riff-
raff they attracted.

A more familiar use of poetry in a contest that might
involve gambling has been known from the seventeenth
century as *karuta*. The two halves of poems from the thir-
teenth-century anthology *Hyakunin Isshu* (One Hundred
Poems by One Hundred Poets) are inscribed on separate
cards. Those cards with the first half of the poems are read
aloud by the person who presides over the gathering, and
the contestants search through the remaining cards, placed
face-up on the table, to find the second halves of the poems.
The object is to identify and snatch away as many cards as
possible. To get a jump on the other players, this requires
an ability to recognize each of the hundred poems by the
first few syllables. The popularity of this game, which continues to our day, has insured that most Japanese are familiar with at least the one hundred poems of the game, even if
they know no other poetry.

A variation on this game is the *iroha karuta*, a set of
forty-eight maxims, some versified proverbs, which are divided into first and second parts. When the first part of one
of the selections is read aloud, the participants search the
table for the second half. This game was invented in the
middle of the nineteenth century, and the proverbs themselves, thanks to the game, are known to virtually every
Japanese today.

It may seem inappropriate that poetry should be used for
games that sometimes involve gambling, but the connec-
tions between poetry and money became quite overt during
the seventeenth and eighteenth centuries. The principal po-

etic form at this time was the haiku, and haiku masters made their living mainly by correcting the poetry of their pupils. Earlier poets like the renga master Sōgi had traveled around the country, staying for months at a time with the local potentates in return for graciously condescending to composing renga with them; but in the *kinsei* period (1600–1867), haiku masters were less likely to receive hospitality than a monetary payment for each poem corrected. Of course, a poet had to be established as a recognized master before people would pay for corrections. Bashō, the greatest of the haiku masters, was an exception in that he did not depend on correction fees, but lived from the sale of his calligraphy and gifts from his devoted pupils. After Bashō's death various pupils insisted that they had received secret instructions from him, though in his lifetime he had never spoken of secrets; or they quoted conversations during which Bashō allegedly had declared that only that pupil *really* understood his master's poetry. This was one way poets had of enhancing their prestige and of increasing the number of paying pupils. For such men the chief use of the haiku was as a means of assuring their daily rice. The commercialization of the haiku continued during the kinsei period; and soon after the Meiji Restoration of 1868 one haiku master hit on the idea of installing a large box outside his house into which busy pupils could deposit their haiku along with a flat correction fee of eight *mon* per poem. In our own day students of haiku still pay their teachers for the privilege of attending monthly meetings at which poems by the disciples are discussed, and for receiving the magazine, published by the group, in which their own poems may occasionally be printed.

After the end of World War II, poetry, especially the traditional forms such as the tanka and haiku, was attacked as being without use, as merely a polite diversion without intrinsic literary merit. In 1946 Professor Kuwabara Takeo of Kyoto University published a famous essay in which he asserted that haiku was a second-rate art. Using methodology similar to that of I. A. Richards in *Practical Criticism*, Kuwabara asked various people to rate a number of haiku, concealing the names of the poets. The answers were so chaotic—poems that had appeared in the Postman's Gazette or the Butcher's Companion were not infrequently rated higher than those by acknowledged masters—that he concluded that there simply were no standards when it came to judging haiku except the reputations of the poets.

Undoubtedly the importance of some haiku can be instantly recognized only by persons who are themselves expert practitioners; but Kuwabara's analysis, based on the assumption that *any* educated reader should be able to distinguish literary quality, nevertheless hit the mark so effectively that many aspiring haiku poets abandoned an art which had been thus stigmatized. But many more people kept up with their haiku, indifferent to such criticisms. For them it was of no importance whether the art they practiced was first or second rate. The use they made of it was to cultivate the creative impulses that arose within them, in a form ideally suited to impromptu composition, though also extremely demanding at the highest level. Japanese who feel dissatisfied with the conventions and restrictions of the haiku or of the tanka may turn to composing poetry in modern forms, and this has approximately the same uses as poetry composed elsewhere in the world.

Many distinctive uses of Japanese poetry have atrophied or even totally disappeared. But whenever I give a lecture somewhere in Japan and am confronted at its end with people who come up to me with squares of cardboard on which I am expected to inscribe poems of my own composition, I realize that some traditional uses of poetry survive and contribute to the uniqueness of Japanese culture today.

FOUR ■

JAPANESE
FICTION

IN JAPAN, as in many other countries, poetry was composed before literary prose. The eighth-century *Kojiki* has its admirers who insist on the simple strength of the narration, but because of the peculiar writing system that was employed in it, nobody really knows whether it should be read as Japanese or as bad Chinese with occasional intrusions of Japanese words. All the other early examples of prose are either in unmistakable Chinese or else in the same kind of adulterous mélange of Japanese and Chinese that is characteristic of the *Kojiki*.

The first example of sustained Japanese literary prose is the preface to the *Kokinshū* written by Ki no Tsurayuki in 905. Years ago, when I began to teach at Cambridge University, I discovered that undergraduates who were reading Japanese began their studies with the preface to the *Kokinshū*. I was astonished to learn this; I had always assumed that one began Japanese, like any other living language, with conversational phrases, such as the usual inquiries after the pen of one's aunt. But the tradition of classics was strong at Cambridge, and it was natural for an undergraduate there to learn a language that he would never dream of speaking. Eventually I decided that the preface to the *Kokinshū* was not a bad choice: it is beautifully composed, has a limited vocabulary, absolutely regular grammar, and very few Chinese characters.

Ki no Tsurayuki is also remembered for the *Tosa Nikki* (Tosa Diary) in which he described his return journey in 935 to Kyoto from the province of Tosa, where he had been serving as the governor. The work begins, "Diaries are things written by men, I am told. I am writing this to show what a woman can do." These opening lines are obviously untrue, but it was not unusual for men to write poems in the persona of a woman, and Tsurayuki simply made the same pretense in his diary, probably in order to explain why it was written in Japanese rather than in classical Chinese, the language in which men at the court normally wrote. He does not reveal why he chose to write in Japanese, but we may conjecture that it was because he wished to describe a personal experience that could be conveyed adequately only in his native tongue, not in a language learned at school. The experience in question was the death of his daughter in Tosa, a tragedy to which he refers again and again, always in his adopted persona of a gentlewoman in the governor's entourage.

It is likely that at least two surviving works of fiction antedate the *Tosa Diary*, though we have no firm dates for either. The first, *Taketori Monogatari* (The Tale of the Bamboo Cutter), is the oldest surviving example of the *monogatari*, a word that means literally "a telling of things." Some scholars date it 910, about five years after the compilation of the *Kokinshū*. Perhaps it was originally composed in a mixture of Chinese and Japanese, as scholars have long suggested, but the present text is in kana, with only about one hundred words of Chinese origin.

The Tale of the Bamboo Cutter has been known as "the ancestor of all romances" ever since Murasaki Shikibu so described it in *The Tale of Genji*. She added, "The story has been with us for a very long time, as familiar as the bamboo growing before us." Despite its title, it is the story of the beautiful Kaguya-hime, and not of the Bamboo Cutter, who serves mainly to open and close the tale. The old Bamboo Cutter and his wife, we are told, had long lived in poverty and were childless. One day the Bamboo Cutter found a stalk of bamboo that gave forth light and discovered inside it a tiny little girl whom he took home with him. Like bamboo, within three months she shot up to full height, and word spread of her extraordinary beauty. Suitors called to express their desire to marry her, but she refused even to see them. In the end only five men persisted despite the rebuffs, and at the urging of the Bamboo Cutter, who reminded Kaguya-hime that in this world people customarily marry, she agreed to marry whichever of the suitors performed the task she imposed on him. She demanded that they bring back such rare items as the stone begging bowl the Buddha himself had carried, a fur robe that would not burn in fire, and the jewel from the head of a sea dragon. All five men ultimately failed in their tasks, to the boundless delight of Kaguya-hime, who had no intention of marrying. The Emperor, however, also learned of Kaguya-hime's beauty, and with the connivance of the Bamboo Cutter, visited her house while on a hunt. Unable either to refuse or accept the Emperor, Kaguya-hime turned herself into a pool of light, demonstrating that she was a supernatural being, and the Emperor abandoned his suit.

After three years had gone by in this manner, Kaguya-hime became increasingly pensive and spent much of her time gazing at the moon. One night she burst into tears and revealed to the old Bamboo Cutter that she was not a creature of this world but had come originally from the Palace of the Moon. Soon, she predicted, people from the moon would come to fetch her. Sure enough, a flying chariot arrived from the moon. The Bamboo Cutter tried to prevent the moon people from taking Kaguya-hime away, but he could not resist their otherworldly powers. Before donning a robe of feathers that would take away all memory of this world, she offered a jar of the elixir of immortality to the old man and his wife; but now that Kaguya-hime was lost to them, they no longer desired to remain in this world, and they refused it. She offered the elixir then to the Emperor, who also refused, because he would not be able to see Kaguya-hime again. He commanded a messenger to place the elixir atop the highest mountain in the land and set it afire. The tale concludes, "Ever since they burnt the elixir of immortality on its summit people have called the mountain Fuji, meaning immortal. Even now the smoke still rises into the clouds."

The tale has been analyzed into five component parts: the girl born inside a bamboo stalk and her rapid growth; the courtship of the five suitors and their adventures; the visit of the Emperor; Kaguya-hime's putting on the robe of feathers and returning to the moon; and the smoke rising over Mount Fuji. Each of these themes has precedents or parallels in the folklore of Asia. The most striking resemblances are to a Tibetan folktale first recorded by a Chinese scholar in 1954. The similarities between this story and *The Tale of the Bamboo Cutter* are so striking that when the Tibetan tale was published in Japan, many scholars immediately accepted

it as evidence that the oldest work of Japanese fiction had
originated in the borderland between China and Tibet. However, the lack of any similar tale elsewhere in China and the
extremely close resemblances between a Japanese text of the
ninth century and a Tibetan folktale related over a thousand
years later suggested to other scholars that some Japanese—
perhaps one of the military who infiltrated the area in the
early 1920s—had passed the story on to the Tibetans.

Some elements in the story, such as the tests administered
to the suitors, who probably numbered only three originally, are found in folktales known all over the world. One
recalls the three caskets in *The Merchant of Venice,* or the
three suitors of the stony-hearted Princess Turandot. But
The Tale of the Bamboo Cutter is conspicuously distinguished from folktales by the attitude of the narrator toward
the characters. The satire directed against the unlucky suitors is unusual, but the literary interest of the tale stems
mostly from the characterization of the Bamboo Cutter and
Kaguya-hime. The Bamboo Cutter is a rather dim-witted
man who, by the accident of having found a girl in a stalk of
bamboo, manages to rise in the world. His wisdom is com-
monsensical: when Kaguya-hime reaches a suitable age, she
should get married like any other girl. It does not occur to
him that someone found in a bamboo stalk might be an
exception to this general rule. He is also so guileless that he
does not see what is happening even as Kaguya-hime cold-
bloodedly disposes of one suitor after another. He is so
impressed by the robe of fire-rat fur offered by the Minister
of the Right that he insists on inviting him into the house.
Kaguya-hime attempts to restrain the old man, pointing out
that they have not yet verified that the robe will not burn in
fire, but the Bamboo Cutter answers, "That may be so, but
I'll invite him in anyway. In all the world there is not

another such fur robe. You'd best accept it as genuine. Don't make people suffer so!"

Kaguya-hime fears for a while that the Minister of the Right may actually have been successful in the impossible task she assigned him, but when she tests the robe, it burns brightly in the flames. "Just as I thought," says Kaguya-hime, "the robe was an imitation." The Minister, it is reported, turns the color of leaves of grass, but Kaguya-hime is enchanted.

The cold-heartedness of the beautiful princess is humorously but unmistakably evoked. Perhaps it was by way of satirizing fairy tales then current that the unknown author told again a familiar story. But in our day, ironically, the folktale portrait of Kaguya-hime has been restored: Kaguya-hime now figures in children's books as a lovable creature from another world, and scholars gravely point out that she is unsullied by base, human emotions. Folktales lie behind many early works of Japanese fiction, and they would be utilized again and again over the centuries. For example, the robe of feathers figures prominently in the fifteenth-century Nō play *Hagoromo* and also in the most popular Japanese play written since 1945, *Yūzuru* (Twilight Crane) by Kinoshita Junji.

Another, quite different tradition of fiction also originated in the late ninth or early tenth century, the *uta monogatari*, or "poem tales." Even works of straightforward narration like *The Tale of the Bamboo Cutter* contained poetry, included as an integral part of the experiences of the characters, but the poem tales are constructed around the poems they contain. The successive episodes of a poem tale explain different, often unrelated poems, and the episodes themselves are likely to be unconnected, not forming a cohesive narrative. The most celebrated by far of the poem tales is *Ise*

Monogatari (Tales of Ise). Along with the *Kokinshū* it exercised the greatest influence on later Japanese literature of any work of the Heian period, and innumerable manuscripts survive, many of them illustrated. It may seem strange that a work consisting of 125 episodes only casually connected, which at times are no more than bare explanations of where and when a poem was composed, should have possessed such an enormous appeal. *The Tale of Genji* is a far more impressive work, but perhaps its length militated against its wide circulation. The brief episodes of *Tales of Ise*, whether taken individually or read together, made fewer demands on readers, who no doubt enjoyed getting in encapsulated form its glimpses of the glamour of the Heian court. Later generations looked back to the period it evokes as a golden age to be emulated, though without much hope of ever attaining its glory.

We do not know who wrote *Tales of Ise*. Probably there was no single author who at a particular time sat down and set about composing the work. Perhaps the unnamed hero of most of the episodes, who has been identified as Ariwara no Narihira (825–880), himself wrote the earliest version, which contained poems that he and people around him had composed on various occasions, together with explanations —not necessarily truthful—of the circumstances. The briefness and ambiguity of these waka often made them difficult to understand, and people were no doubt curious about the personal life of Narihira, known as a great lover. The poems in *Tales of Ise* benefit immensely from their prose settings. Even the most puzzling of Narihira's poems becomes intelligible in its context. This is episode 4:

Long ago an Empress Dowager was residing at Gojō in the eastern part of the capital, and a certain woman lived in the western wing of her house. A man who at first had no such intentions fell madly in love with the woman and visited her there, but around the tenth day of the first month the woman disappeared. He later discovered where she was, but it was not a place ordinary people could visit, and this caused him all the greater torment.

In the first month of the following year, when the plum blossoms were at their height, he remembered their love of the year before and went to her house. He looked at the place standing, then sat down to look at it again, but it did not seem in the least as it had a year earlier, no matter from which angle he viewed it. He burst into tears, then lay on the bare wooden floor until the moon sank in the sky. Remembering the events of the previous year, he composed this poem:

> *tsuki ya aranu*
> *haru ya mukashi no*
> *haru naranu*
> *wagami hitotsu wa*
> *moto no mi ni shite*

> Is that not the moon?
> And is the spring not the spring
> Of a year ago?
> This body of mine alone
> Remains as it was before.

Even as he composed this poem the sky gradually grew light and he left, weeping bitterly.

In the poem Narihira seems to be asking rhetorically if the moon is the same one that he and his beloved saw the year before, and if the spring is the same spring. But if the questions are rhetorical, why does he claim that he alone remains unchanged? If the questions are not rhetorical, and he really is not sure whether it is the same moon and the same spring, his claim that he alone is unchanged is easier to follow, but it goes against common sense. The poem is difficult to understand, and there is no authoritative explanation, but the context in *Tales of Ise* makes the meaning clearer: he is in the same room where just a year ago he met the woman he loves, yet everything looks different. It is possible to doubt that the moon is the same moon; perhaps the spring is not the same spring as a year before; but it is impossible to doubt that he is the same person and is still moved by the same love.

Tales of Ise has been interpreted as an example of the Japanese nostalgia for the past, a desperate attempt to halt the flow of time by preserving from oblivion poignant moments in the life of a poet. The work has also been read as a kind of biography: it opens with an account of how, when Narihira had barely come of age, he caught a glimpse of two beautiful young sisters and addressed a poem to them; and it concludes with the poem he wrote when he sensed that death was near. But no attempt was made to keep the in-between episodes in chronological order, and many are clearly not about Narihira. Surely there is an element of fiction even in the parts that seem closest to fact.

Although it is obvious that *Tales of Ise* shares very little with *The Tale of the Bamboo Cutter*, each belonged to the court traditions of roughly the same period, and each established a tradition of fiction. *The Tale of Genji*, the supreme work of Japanese fiction, owes much to both traditions, as well as to collections of waka and the diaries of court ladies. It resembles *The Tale of the Bamboo Cutter* in relating a single story chronologically and in subordinating the poetry to the prose, and it follows *Tales of Ise* in giving vignettes of life at the court.

It has been conjectured from an entry in Murasaki's own

diary and various other scraps of information that she began writing her novel between 1001, the year her husband died, and 1005, when she entered the service of the Empress Shōshi, and the work was probably completed by 1010. We know from mention in *Sarashina Nikki* (As I Crossed a Bridge of Dreams) that not only was the whole of *The Tale of Genji* completed by 1021, but the work was known by then even in distant provinces. Its high reputation at the court is attested to by the command of the Emperor Ichijō that it be read to him, though men at the court normally scorned anything composed in Japanese.

The first germs of *The Tale of Genji* may have been the tales of court life of the past, similar to those in *Tales of Ise*, related to the ladies of the court by some gentlewoman for their diversion. Perhaps Murasaki depended on a scenario that gave the essential facts, but she doubtless extemporized in free sections of the narration. Some passages in the present text of *The Tale of Genji* suggest her presence: "I have no doubt that there were many fine passages in the letters with which he saddened the lives of his many ladies, but grief-stricken myself, I did not listen as carefully as I might have."[1] The narrator is never identified, but she serves to link this highly evolved work with the older traditions of the *monogatari*, "a telling of things."

The Tale of Genji covers a period of about seventy years. Various clues in the text indicate that it opens during the reign of the Emperor Daigo (897–930), a time that people of Murasaki Shikibu's day considered a golden age. It has often been suggested that the model for the Shining Prince Genji was Minamoto no Takaakira (914–982), the tenth son of the Emperor Daigo; not only was he, like Genji, made a com-

1. Murasaki Shikibu, *The Tale of Genji*, Edward G. Seidensticker, trans. (New York: Knopf, 1976), vol. 1, p. 220.

poem, and she makes several references to it, especially at the opening of *The Tale of Genji*, but there are naturally immense differences between a poem in fewer than two hundred lines and a novel that is over one thousand pages long. The search for literary sources has been inspired largely by scholars' difficulty in imagining that a work of the magnitude of *The Tale of Genji* could have been created without models. Many far-fetched sources have been seriously considered, but perhaps the most persuasive interpretation of the novel was made by the eighteenth-century scholar Motoori Norinaga. He wrote,

There have been many interpretations over the years of the purpose of this tale. But all of these interpretations have been based not on a consideration of the novel itself but rather on the novel as seen from the point of view of Confucian and Buddhist works, and thus do not represent the true purpose of the author. . . . Good and evil as found in this tale do not correspond to good and evil as found in Confucian and Buddhist writings. . . . Generally speaking, those who know the meaning of the sorrow of human existence, that is, those who are in sympathy and in harmony with human sentiments are regarded as good; and those who are not aware of the poignance of human existence—those who are not in harmony with human sentiments—are regarded as bad. . . . Man's feelings do not always follow the dictates of his mind. They arise in man in spite of himself and are difficult to control. In the instance of Prince Genji, his interest in and meetings with various women, including the Imperial Consort Fujitsubo, are acts of extraordinary iniquity and immorality according to the Confucian and Buddhist points of view. It would be difficult to call Prince Genji a good man, however numerous his other admirable qualities. But *The Tale of Genji* does not dwell on his iniquities and immoral acts, but rather recites again and again his awareness of the sorrow of existence, and represents him as a good man who combines in himself all good things in men.[2]

Later in the same essay Motoori declares that the purpose of the author of *The Tale of Genji* was similar to that of a man who collects muddy water in which lotuses can be brought to bloom: "The impure mud of the illicit love affairs described in *The Tale of Genji* is there not for the purpose of being admired but for nurturing the flower of the awareness of the sorrow of human existence."

The phrase in the original that has been translated as "the sorrow of human existence" is *mono no aware*. It might better be translated as "a sensitivity to things," but this sensitivity usually takes the form of realizing the perishability of beauty and human happiness. Genji is peerlessly handsome, incomparably gifted in whatever he does— whether painting, dancing, or composing poetry—but he is above all a great lover. This should not suggest that he is another Don Juan. Unlike Don Juan or Don Giovanni in Mozart's opera, he is uninterested in the number of women he conquers; he has no Leporello to record how many in this place or that. And unlike Don Giovanni, who humiliates Donna Elvira for not realizing that their affair is over, Genji never forgets or slights any woman he has loved. Even when he has made a dreadful mistake and courts a grotesque woman because she lives in a romantically overgrown palace and plays old music, he does not abandon her, but moves

2. Motoori Norinaga, "Tama no Ogushi," translated in Ryusaku Tsunoda, Wm. Theodore de Bary, and Donald Keene, *Sources of Japanese Tradition* (New York: Columbia University Press, 1958), pp. 532–535.

her into his great palace. He is sensitive to each woman, different to each, and yet always sincere. He obviously loves this world, but his often-expressed desire to leave it and become a Buddhist priest is not a pretense; above all he is aware of the meaning of *mono no aware.*

Genji dies about two-thirds of the way through the novel. Murasaki Shikibu evidently could not bear describing his death. In her last description of Genji we are told that he looked so beautiful, despite his age (in his forties) and his grief over the death of his beloved wife Murasaki, that an old priest could not restrain his tears. The next chapter opens with the bald statement: "Genji was dead and there was no one to take his place." The last third of the novel describes two young men, one a grandson of Genji, the other supposed by the world to be Genji's son but actually the son of another man. The grandson, Niou, has Genji's charm and success with women, but he is rather heartless; the supposed son, Kaoru, is sensitive, absorbed by religion, but seems incapable of ever winning a woman he loves. Genji has been fragmented into two unusually attractive but incomplete young men, who must have resembled much more closely the actual men of the court in Murasaki's day than the peerless Genji.

The Heian court was weakened by the rise of military powers outside the capital, and in the twelfth century several revolts occurred, each of which diminished the authority of the court. Then, in the year 1181, a war broke out between the two main military families, the Taira and the Minamoto. The earlier revolts are described in chronicles that are of interest, though not widely read. But the struggle between the Taira and the Minamoto became a part of the lives of Japanese for centuries to come, not only of those who read *Heike Monogatari* (The Tale of the Heike), but of illiterates who heard priests, or men dressed like priests, recite the text to musical accompaniment all over the country. The heroes and villains of this war were commemorated in countless ballads and, as we shall see, in many works for the theater. These are the national heroes of Japan. They were not the first to win glory on the battlefield, but an unbroken tradition links them with the present. The heroes of earlier warfare—for example, the eighth-century general Sakanoe no Tamuramaro, who victoriously fought the Ainu along the borders—are remote, not only because of the greater lapse of time but because of the interruption in the martial tradition during the highly civilized Heian period. *The Tale of Genji* has been loved and revered by educated people ever since it was written, but *The Tale of the Heike* is in the blood of the Japanese.

The Tale of the Heike opens with a famous passage telling of the impermanence of all things. Buddhist sentiments were commonly voiced by the characters in *The Tale of Genji*, but, as Motoori noted, the novel is not to be interpreted as a Buddhist allegory. In the case of *The Tale of the Heike*, however, there is an unmistakable Buddhist tone underlying even the descriptions of battles. The first chapters are devoted to the overweening general Taira no Kiyomori, who had seized control of the government after one of the rebellions of the mid-twelfth century. He is a tyrant, in the European manner rather than the usually more subdued Japanese manner. But his glory does not last long: the Taira forces are defeated in battle, and the work concludes with an account of Kenreimon'in, the daughter of Kiyomori and the consort of an emperor, who after the final Taira defeat becomes a nun and lives in poverty at the convent Jakkō-in.

The Tale of the Heike is episodic, superb in parts, dull in others, sometimes wonderfully evocative in its language, sometimes pompous in its invocations of Chinese precedents for the noble or wicked actions described. It lives in terms of the heroes' great moments—the embittered Shunkan, exiled to a remote island for his part in a conspiracy and deserted by his fellow conspirators; Nasu no Yoichi standing on the shore shooting an arrow that squarely hits the fan a Taira court lady on a boat holds up as a target; the death of the young Taira general Atsumori, killed with regret by his enemy; the death of the boy-emperor Antoku, whose nurse carries him under the waves rather than letting him fall into enemy hands. The prevailing tone of the work stems from the defeats and deaths, not from the triumphs; this war tale tells of men who do not wish to kill, of victories that bring no joy.

The Tale of the Heike is sometimes credited to a priest named Kakuichi, but even if he wrote the original version early in the thirteenth century, the work continued to grow during the following centuries as it was embellished by successive reciters. We do not know the names of the authors of the later war tales and other works of fiction written between the thirteenth and seventeenth centuries. These were the Japanese Middle Ages, not quite as dark as our own, but equally turbulent, marked by constant warfare rather than by the refined culture so hauntingly evoked in *The Tale of Genji*. The fiction of the middle ages is colored by Buddhism, not only the kind of Buddhism that one finds in the sacred texts, but by accounts of life in monasteries and stories of miracles and prodigies.

The most typical literary genre of this period was the *renga*, or linked verse, described in chapter 3; several poets took turns in composing "links" to form a chain of poetry. The object of renga composition was not to create a long poem that might have been the work of a single poet, but to combine the different sensibilities of several different poets in a poem that lacks unity but is always smoothly flowing and full of surprises. In order to compose renga successfully it was necessary to have a quick mind that could respond to the verse composed by another person by composing a verse of one's own in the same mood, but distinctive. It was possible to link verses by meaning, carrying forward the thought of the previous poet; by verbal association, sometimes using a word from the preceding poem in a different sense; or by free association, playing upon the overtones evoked on hearing another man's lines.

Usually three or more poets participated in a renga session, but on occasion one man would compose the entire sequence. This became something of a fad by the seventeenth century. In 1675 Ihara Saikaku, who would soon emerge as the first important fiction writer of the period, composed by himself 1,000 verses in one day, at the rate of a verse every thirty-five seconds. In 1677 he raised the total to 1,600; in 1680, in response to the challenge of two other masters of extemporaneous composition, he lifted his total to 4,000 verses in a day; and in 1684 he composed the incredible total of 23,500 verses in a single day and night, too fast for the scribes to do more than tally. These exuberant displays of wit and technique were not meant to last as literature. Like so much of the artistic effort of the late seventeenth century, Saikaku's renga was meant for the present only, for delighting in the rapidly shifting patterns of the "floating world" where waves constantly form and break.

Saikaku's first novel, *Kōshoku Ichidai Otoko* (The Life of an Amorous Man), was published in 1682 and created a new genre. In an impressionistic manner that recalls renga composition, *The Life of an Amorous Man* traces the career of a man from his precocious essays at lovemaking as a child of seven to his decision at the age of sixty to sail on a ship, whose name may be translated the S.S. *Lust*, to an island populated exclusively by women. The name of the hero, Yonosuke, is derived from the word *ukiyo*, "the floating world." Unlike Japanese of the past who looked back nostalgically to some golden age, this hero is interested only in the present, and he shows none of Genji's awareness of "the pity of things." When at the age of thirty-four he is informed of his father's death, he does not spare the time even for a conventional moment of sadness or reflections on the transitory nature of this world. His mother, with an intuitive understanding of what really interests her son, hands him a document transferring to him an immense fortune. Yonosuke cries, "The moment I have waited for so long has come at last! I will ransom all the prostitutes I want, or else I'll buy the services of every last courtesan worthy of the name. Now's my chance!"

In literary terms, *The Life of an Amorous Man* is distinguished chiefly by its style. It opens with a sentence typical of Saikaku's manner when he composed renga: "Sakura mo chiru ni nageki, tsuki wa kagiri arite Irusa-yama." A fairly literal translation would be, "We grieve when cherry blossoms fall, and the moon, having its limits, sinks behind Irusa Mountain." The full meaning, however, is something like: "The sights of nature, such as the cherry blossoms or the moon, give us pleasure, but this pleasure is necessarily of limited duration: the blossoms fall and the moon disappears behind a mountain. But the pleasures of the flesh have no limits." This kind of elliptic utterance owed much to Saikaku's training as a renga poet, and it gave to the rather sordid tale of the hero's amorous exploits an éclat that captivated his readers.

The Life of an Amorous Man sold about one thousand

copies in its first printing, making it a best-seller for those days, and soon there were also pirated editions, one with illustrations by the great Moronobu. This success may have induced Saikaku to consider becoming a professional writer of fiction. In 1685 he wrote his masterpiece, *Kōshoku Gonin Onna* (Five Women Who Loved Love). The stories of the five women are told superbly, with an irony and detachment that do not diminish Saikaku's obvious affection for the characters he observes, as it were, through the reverse end of a telescope. Seen at the distance he has chosen, the antics of the men and women, even their tragic misfortunes, do not excite our pity and terror, but our smiles. Four of the five heroines end unhappily, executed for adultery and other crimes or driven by despair into becoming nuns, but the total effect is not sad. This is the last we hear of one heroine: "Today the name of Osan still brings to mind her beautiful figure, clothed in the pale-blue slip which she wore to her execution."[3]

Saikaku's fiction is generally divided into three groups: stories that treat the amorous affairs of men and women; those that describe with admiration the samurai and their particular code of behavior; and those that depict merchant life, especially in Osaka. The tales about happy and unhappy loves include most of Saikaku's best-known works, and even if nothing else of his work remained, his fame would probably be about the same. When critics say of a work of fiction that it is in the manner of Saikaku, they refer to the epigrammatic brilliance of style and the combination of humor and sensuality typical of the amorous tales. His accounts of the samurai, thought not without interest, are generally

---

3. Ihara Saikaku, *Five Women Who Loved Love*, Wm. Theodore de Bary, trans. (Rutland, Vt.: Tuttle, 1956), p. 156.

lacking in his characteristic humor; he was evidently fasci-
nated by this class, which was distinctly not his own, but he
was unconvincing when he attempted to demonstrate how
superior to ordinary mortals samurai were in their obedi-
ence to a code that demanded extraordinary acts of ven-
geance and self-sacrifice. The tales about the merchant class
—most of them descriptions either of how hard work and
intelligence enable even desperately poor men to become
rich, or how addiction to the extravagances of the upper
classes causes merchants to lose their fortunes—are not only
more interesting, but have sometimes been cited as evidence
of Saikaku's dissatisfaction with the political and economic
situation in the Japan of his day. One can equally well find
evidence to support the opposite view in such typical adages
as "Poverty never catches up to the hard worker." Obviously Saikaku had no consistent philosophy but was inex-
haustibly interested in the human comedy, and he knew
how to communicate his observations in a style that owed
much to his background as a poet of comic renga, and that
was perfectly suited in tempo and suggestiveness to the
narration of his tales.

The influence of Saikaku is easily detected in the *ukiyo
zōshi*, or "stories of the floating world," which constituted
the mainstream of Japanese fiction during the early eighteenth century. One writer, Miyako no Nishiki by name,
borrowed so liberally from Saikaku that he felt he had to
defend himself against the charge of plagiarism. He pain-
stakingly pointed out examples of plagiarism from both
Chinese and Japanese literature to demonstrate that it was
normal and even admirable, concluding, "One can see,
therefore, that Miyako no Nishiki is guilty of no great sin if
he used in his compositions words hastily tossed off by
Saikaku. To take old materials and make them new is the

work of a master." Other writers of the time, perhaps thicker-skinned than Miyako no Nishiki, tranquilly borrowed passages and even whole stories from Saikaku without feeling the need to justify their actions.

During the latter part of the eighteenth century the center of literary composition shifted from the Kyoto-Osaka region to Edo, the shogun's capital. The fiction written from then until the country was opened to literary influences from the West after the Meiji Restoration of 1868 is generally known as *gesaku*. The term means "playful composition," but this refers not to the nature of the work itself but to the attitude of the author. Some of the gesaku writers belonged to the samurai class and allowed their names to appear on frivolous writings only after making it clear that they themselves did not take seriously these accounts of the denizens of the licensed quarters and of similar people who were unworthy of the attention of a gentleman-scholar.

The literary training received by the samurai had traditionally been focused on the Chinese classics, not only the works of Confucius but the poetry of the distant past. During the kinsei period, however, under the influence of the great scholar of Neo-Confucianism Ogyū Sorai, some samurai also learned colloquial Chinese. For the first time Chinese novels and stories of recent dynasties written in the colloquial came to influence Japanese literature. The 1776 collection *Ugetsu Monogatari* (Tales of Rain and the Moon) by the most important novelist of the century after Saikaku, Ueda Akinari, revealed the pervasiveness of this new Chinese influence. Akinari did not merely translate or adapt Chinese originals, but rewrote them so brilliantly that they are usually far more effective as literature than the originals.

Gesaku included not only humorous or merely entertaining works but also long novels of obvious didactic intent.

The last fiction writer before the Meiji Restoration, Takizawa Bakin, began his career with the usual frivolous accounts of doings in the licensed quarters, but his fame is based on the works of his maturity, notably *Nansō Satomi Hakkenden* (Biographies of the Eight Dogs of Satomi)—a title which sounds less ridiculous in the original than in translation. This long work, over which Bakin labored from 1814 to 1841, describes eight young men who have the world *inu*, or "dog," in their surnames. They are all the spiritual heirs of the same noble dog, but each is the embodiment of a particular Confucian virtue. The popularity of the book was largely thanks to the adventures and prodigies narrated in the course of describing how the heroes resisted temptation or overcame dangers, but Bakin included these episodes mainly as a sugar coating that would induce readers to swallow the medicine of the Confucian lessons at the heart of his work.

By the end of his career, even the prodigiously gifted Bakin seemed to have exhausted the possibilities of gesaku literature, and the middle of the nineteenth century was a dreary period for Japanese fiction as a whole. If we can believe contemporary accounts, by the early 1870s not more than five men were making a living as writers of fiction. The scarcity of writers may have been somewhat exaggerated, but there is no way to exaggerate the unreadability of the fiction being written at the time. The great tradition of the Japanese novel seemed to have come to an end. A revival might conceivably have occurred even without the introduction from the West of new models of literature, but this particular stimulus, transmitted to the Japanese in the form of translations and adaptations, in fact led to the creation of a new kind of Japanese fiction, one that is now read all over the world.

FIVE ■

JAPANESE THEATER

JAPANESE THEATER is one of the richest in the world. It is possible today on a typical Sunday in, say, October to find a performance of Nō, a distinctive form of drama perfected in the fourteenth century, at three or four Tokyo theaters; of Kabuki, a form of drama evolved in the seventeenth century, at at least two theaters; as well as various forms of modern theater, both works written by Japanese in the twentieth century and foreign plays and musicals in Japanese translation. If one is lucky—though it is by no means rare—there will be performances at the National Theater of Bunraku, the puppet drama, and sometimes specially arranged performances of *bugaku,* the oldest surviving form of Japanese theatrical entertainment, dating back to the eighth century. Moreover, the real aficionado of Japanese theater need not be content with what is available in Tokyo alone, although one can find there an extraordinary variety of spectacles throughout the year; he or she can visit remote parts of Japan where almost forgotten theatricals of long ago have been miraculously preserved. Indeed, one can say without exaggeration that every form of play or dance known since the seventh century survives somewhere, at least vestigially.

The earliest kind of performances recorded in writing are of *gigaku*, a kind of dance with mimetic elements imported from China in 612 A.D. Undoubtedly other kinds of dance, performed at Shintō shrines or at festivals, antedate gigaku, but in the absence of records we do not know exactly when or how they were performed. The *Kojiki* contains the story of the time when the sun goddess Amaterasu, angry over her brother's defilement of her weaving hall, shut herself up in a cave and plunged the world into darkness. Another goddess, hoping to lure Amaterasu from the cave, performed a lascivious dance that evoked laughter from the assembled gods. Curious to see what they were laughing about, Amaterasu stuck her head out of the cave, whereupon a strong-armed god dragged her forth and made her promise never to hide again. This episode used to be cited with the utmost seriousness by scholars of Japanese theater as the inception of the art; but the account of the lascivious dance is disappointingly brief.

More substantial evidence remains concerning the early history of gigaku. Several hundred gigaku masks have been preserved, and they indicate that the performers appeared as animals, birds, strange foreigners, men of prodigious strength, and so on. One gigaku entertainment that is still performed is the *shishimai*, or lion dance, a popular feature of many festivals.

A gigaku performance apparently began with the procession of the various masked personages, followed by dances that were accompanied by flutes and drums. Some dances had mimetic elements; for example, the actor masked and attired as a bird might pretend to be pecking for worms. The prevailing tone was cheerful, perhaps even funny, but no doubt the Japanese performed them with considerable gravity, if only because they originated in China, a land respected as the fountainhead of culture. The ceremonies performed when the Great Image of the Buddha was dedicated in 752 at the Tōdaiji, the magnificent temple in Nara, were the high point in the history of gigaku. Sixty gigaku performers appeared on this occasion, but half a century later only two men were recorded as being qualified gigaku artists.

The court in the meantime had discovered a more decorous entertainment, the stately dances of *bugaku*, and the gigaku performers were no longer in demand. Bugaku dances are still performed at the Imperial Palace in Tokyo and at major Shintō shrines, much as they have been performed for over a millennium. No doubt changes have occurred imperceptibly over the years, and some dances are clearly of Japanese origin, but as a whole they retain a distinctly alien atmosphere, not so much Chinese as Central Asian or perhaps even Indian. The masks, unique to bugaku, are sometimes bright red with long noses, sometimes half-human and half-animal, sometimes the faces of weird imaginary animals that combine the attributes of birds and beasts. The costumes and headdresses are also exotic—brilliantly colored robes with long trains, elaborate hats or hoods in the shapes of the plumage of birds or curved like helmets, or flowing hoods three feet long that drape down the dancer's back. But above all, the music (called *gagaku*) creates the special atmosphere associated with bugaku. It is the only orchestral music of Japan, combining strings, woodwinds, drums, and gongs. The *shō*, a kind of panpipe, and the *hichiriki*, a piercingly high flute, typify gagaku to most people; but the *biwa*, a kind of lute, and the huge gagaku drum, flame-shaped and taller than a man, are no less typical. The effect produced by the gagaku orchestra is strangely moving, even to people who usually do not like any form of East Asian music. Gagaku is unique, moreover, in that no words are sung to it, though in every other form of music for the theater in Japan words are indispensable.

To see a performance of bugaku at some shrine, preferably by moonlight, is an unforgettable experience. The otherworldly sound of the music; the crunch of the wooden shoes of the dancers on the gravel of the inner courtyard of a shrine pavilion; the colors of the costumes, masks, and hoods in the moonlight or torchlight; the slow, somehow significant movements of the dancers cannot fail to stir even the most blasé theatergoer. But bugaku in brilliant sunlight, say on the stage of the great shrine at Miyajima built on a platform over the waters of the Inland Sea, is hardly less impressive.

Some bugaku dances have rudimentary plots. One popular piece, *Ranryōō*, is said to concern a Chinese warrior who was so handsome that his face failed to inspire fear in his enemies, so he wore a frightening dragon mask and was easily victorious; but no one seeing the dance today would guess the plot. Another bugaku dance portrays four drunken divinities, and even if the plot is obscure, the movements are eloquent enough to convey their inebriated condition.

Later Japanese theater made use of the heritage of gagaku music and bugaku dances infrequently, most often to suggest the special sacred atmosphere of a shrine. But one principle behind the composition of the playlets would be carefully observed, especially in Nō: the division into three sections of increasingly rapid tempo. Both bugaku pieces and Nō plays open with a *jo* or introductory section that is slow and deliberate in pace; it is followed by the *ha* or development section, much longer and more mimetic, as well as somewhat faster; and they conclude with the *kyū* or fast section, about the same length as the introduction. A person seeing bugaku or Nō for the first time is not likely to be dazzled by the speed of the final section, but to someone attuned to the characteristic tempos of works that a thousand years ago were already ceremonial in nature and performed only in places of special holiness, the final section may indeed appear frenetically rapid.

At about the same time that bugaku was imported from the Asian continent, other, less elevated entertainments also entered Japan—acrobatics, juggling, magical tricks, and so on. Some of these sideshows in time acquired dramatic interest. From the twelfth century we have one-sentence descriptions of playlets such as "The head clerk of a temple slips on the ice and loses his trousers" and "The nun Myōkō begs for swaddling clothes," presumably satirical pieces making fun of the Buddhist clergy.

Records indicate that by the twelfth century, *Okina*, the oldest play in the Nō repertory, was already being performed. The play contains elements derived not only from the kinds of theater I have described but from obscurer rituals and dances of both native and foreign origin. *Okina* stands apart from the rest of the Nō repertory, not only because of its antiquity but because the masks, costumes, and dances are unique to this one play. Before a performance of *Okina* begins, the mask to be worn by the *shite*, or chief character, is displayed in the actors' dressing room and honored with reverent salutations. The actors partake of an extremely simple, ritual meal, and then file out onto the stage and take their places. One actor, called the Mask Bearer, removes the *Okina* mask from its case and offers it to the *shite,* who prostrates himself before accepting it. It is the only Nō play in which the actor puts on his mask in full view of the audience. The *Okina* mask has the features of a benevolent old man, not some fearsome divinity, but they are nonetheless a god's; and although the role is devoid of emotion or special displays of technique, performing it is considered to be so arduous as to shorten the life of the actor.

These aspects of contemporary performances of *Okina* plainly indicate the religious, specifically Shintō origins of the art, in contrast with the secular background of bugaku. There is a legend that Nō originated at the Kasuga Shrine in Nara, where an old man was once seen performing a dance beneath the Yōgō Pine. The old man then revealed that he was a god, and from that time on his memory has been honored at the annual festival of the shine by a Nō actor dancing beneath the pine. The pine is also depicted in the painting that decorates the back wall of the Nō stage and provides the only setting for all Nō plays, regardless of subject.

Okina opens with a series of meaningless syllables (scholars have tried in vain for centuries to make sense of them) that are said to be the utterance of the god who showed himself beneath the Yōgō Pine. The actor, like a medium transmitting words from another world, pronounces words whose meaning is less important than their source. Unlike most Nō plays, *Okina* is not in the least tragic. Insofar as it can be understood, it is a joyous celebration of abundance and long life, but the presence of the god exhausts the actor. And even though an audience would be hard put after a performance of the play to say what happened, the aftertaste is good. *Okina* is perhaps the most widely performed play of the Nō repertory: at the New Year, on important occasions, at festivals even in villages, *Okina* usually opens the program. No one would dream of omitting it; *Okina* is an initiation into the world of Nō.

The solemnity of Nō is what most distinguishes it from other forms of drama. The Japanese enjoy laughing at comedies. Indeed, farces called *Kyōgen* have traditionally been performed between the Nō tragedies. The cheerful mask of the *Okina* actor has suggested to Japanese critics that originally it was a festive, perhaps even comic work, not the stately ceremonial it is today. But whatever the ancient manner of presentation may have been, even a Nō that ends happily is performed today with the deliberation and gravity reserved in most parts of the world for funeral rites. The plays are filled with tragic incidents, and on the rare occasions when a character says "How happy I am!" (*Ureshi ya*) he sounds to the uninitiated spectator like a tortured soul.

The special atmosphere can be detected as soon as one sets foot inside a Nō theater. Before a play there is none of the usual chatter of the audience, even though no one admonishes talkers. The great gleaming expanse of the stage imposes silence, almost like an altar. This is not true of performances of Nō in the countryside, where the audiences, rather like those in Southeast Asia, talk, eat, or doze throughout the plays, or even throw money to actors they admire. Initially, however, the Nō plays may have been performed by the priests of a Shintō shrine, not for a human audience but to please the gods by acting out their miracles or the history of their shrines. At the front of the Nō stage are three steps leading down to ground level. These steps have no function in present-day performances, but no stage is without them. Originally they may have been used by the priests to pass from the shrine to the stage, where they performed for the gods alone. Plays staged to please the gods, even if no human audience watches, are still performed in parts of Southeast Asia; and at the major Shintō shrines such as the Great Shrine of Ise, worshippers pay for dances called *kagura*, not for their own pleasure (though they often do enjoy the dances) but in the hopes of receiving divine favor.

The entertainment offered in a Nō theater is unlikely to amuse the casual visitor. The plays are sung or declaimed in medieval Japanese that is so difficult to understand that even well-educated Japanese in the audience follow the plays with libretti if they have not learned them by heart. There is little movement on the stage until the final dance of the shite that epitomizes his emotions, and there are even a few plays with virtually no action, in which the shite enters, sits in the center of the stage, and then relates his or her tragedy. All roles in professional performances of Nō are taken by men, though there are skilled women amateurs. When a man performs the role of a woman he in no way seeks to imitate the voice, walk, or gestures of a real woman; that would be contemptuously rejected as *shibai*, or "theatricals," by the actors and aficionados. When in an amateur performance a woman plays the part of a woman, the high pitch of her normal voice sounds unnatural, even weird, to people accustomed to hearing men in the roles.

The rejection of realism is perhaps the most conspicuous feature of Nō. Some spectators who are accustomed to other types of dramatic art are never able to accept the demands made on the audience by such theater, but others, even if they have had no previous acquaintance with Nō, are spellbound, rejoicing in the special world into which they have been led. The masks of Nō, its most distinctive visual feature, may originally have been intended to promote realism by giving an actor with an ordinary face the appearance of a beautiful woman, an imposing general, or a fearsome deity; but this realistic aspect of the masks tends to be forgotten today. Newcomers to Nō are more likely to notice that the mask is too small to cover the actor's face, leaving visible a disillusioning fringe of sallow jowls or a chin that literally doubles that of the mask. It would be perfectly simple to make masks big enough to cover the actor's entire face, but apart from the matter of tradition in masks, there is an aesthetic preference for small heads on big bodies that runs counter to the physical reality of big heads on small bodies that characterized most Japanese until recent time.

The costumes of Nō represent another instance of the rejection of realism. Who would guess on seeing the magnificent robes worn by the shite and *tsure* (companion) in the play *Matsukaze* that the two women are supposed to be fisher girls who make a living by dipping salt water from the sea and boiling it to make salt? The discolored rags that fisher girls of the medieval period actually wore would be unthinkable on the Nō stage, where the creation of beauty is always of paramount concern.

Nō, as I have suggested, was originally performed at Shintō shrines by priests. Later, companies of itinerant actors performed in the place of the priests, perhaps because worshippers, once having seen and heard skillful performers, preferred them to priests and were willing to pay to see them. The most important event in the development of Nō as an art occurred in 1374, when the youthful shogun Yoshimitsu attended a performance of Nō at the Imakumano Shrine in Kyoto. This was the first time he had even seen Nō and he was entranced, particularly by the boy actor Zeami, then eleven years old. He decided to accord his patronage to Nō, and the company, which had hitherto traveled from shrine to shrine all over the country wherever there was a local ival, was able to remain in the capital. More important, support meant that instead of attempting to please rus- with exciting or amusing plays, the actors—who were also the dramatists, the choreographers, and the composers —could devote themselves to pleasing an aristocratic audience of connoisseurs.

The texts of Nō, which had hitherto had been fairly close to ordinary conversation, were embellished with quotations from poetry, and the expression was made deliberately ambiguous and multilayered. An audience of connoisseurs could follow even complicated wordplay or allusion. Overt action was rejected in favor of symbolic gesture. The props were reduced to miniatures or bare outlines of the things they represented. For example, in *Matsukaze* the cart laden with pails of brine that the sisters pull (and complain of pulling) is hardly bigger than a toy. A boat is represented by two thin strips of wood joined at the ends, and the area of the boat itself is often so restricted that some of the passengers must ride outside. The costumes and masks were also stylized. There is a phrase in modern Japanese that translates as "a face like a Nō mask," meaning a face devoid of all expression. It is obvious that a mask must be neutral in appearance if it is to be used throughout an entire role that embodies various contrasting emotions, but probably Yoshimitsu and his court also preferred stylized features to realistic depiction. The oldest surviving Nō masks have more individuality of expression than any used today.

Nō developed as the official entertainment of the shogun's court. Zeami, as he matured as both actor and dramatist, rejoiced in the appreciation of his art demonstrated by Yoshimitsu. Unlike the many writers who have predicted that their works would not be fully appreciated until many years had passed, Zeami feared that audiences of the future might not be able to understand plays written for so superior a patron. Indeed, Nō developed into a form of drama that seems to defy even the most commonly accepted axioms of theater.

For example, we are often told that all drama originates in conflict, but there is nothing resembling a conflict in most of the plays of the Nō repertory. Many plays open with the *waki*, or man at the side, entering and informing us that he is a wandering monk who has never seen some part of the country and intends to go there now. He takes a few steps back and then to stage front again, and announces that because he has hurried he is already at his destination. Soon afterwards his attention is caught by a curiously shaped pine, by a girl who has come to offer flowers at a deserted shrine, or by a boy sweeping a garden who responds to the monk's questions in a somehow intriguing manner. The monk may summon a villager to ask him about the pine, or he may directly ask the people he encounters who they are and why they have come to this place, the kind of questions that we in the audience might ask. Bit by bit he learns that this is the spot where, many years ago, two unhappy sisters once lived, or that the lonely shrine is one that Prince Genji visited long ago, or that the boy is actually a god.

There is never any suggestion of conflict between the priest and the ghosts from the past. He may withdraw to the side (befitting his name of "man to the side") and merely listen to the monologue of the shite, or he may promise the anguished soul of some betrayed woman or defeated warrior that he will pray for their repose and pray especially that they may be freed from their attachment to this world, which makes them keep returning and reopening their old wounds. The beautiful play *Nonomiya* (The Shrine in the Fields) is based, like many other works in the Nō

repertory, on *The Tale of Genji*. Lady Rokujō, who appears
in other plays as the demonic presence who kills Genji's wife
Aoi, is here a woman who cannot forget Genji and keeps
coming back to this world to relive her moments with him.
Their last meeting was at the lonely shrine in the fields
outside the capital to which she had accompanied her daughter, who was going to be the new High Priestess of the great
shrine at Ise. The itinerant priest notices a girl who comes
to offer a twig of *sakaki*, the sacred tree of Shintō, at the
deserted shrine. These are her opening words:

> Shrine in the Fields
> Where I have lived with flowers;
> Shrine in the Fields
> Where I have lived with flowers—
> What will be left when autumn has passed?
> Now lonely autumn ends,
> But still my sleeves
> Wilt in a dew of tears;
> The dust racks my body,
> And my heart of itself
> Takes on the fading colors
> Of the thousand flowers;
> It withers, as all things, with neglect.
>
> Each year on this day,
> Unknown to anyone else,
> I return to the old remains.
> In the wood at the Shrine in the Fields
> Autumn has drawn to a close
> And the harsh winds blow.
> Colors so brilliant
> They pierced the senses
> Have faded and vanished;
> What remains now to recall

The memories of the past?
What use was it to come here?
Ahh—how I loathe the attachment
That makes me go back and forth,
Again and again on my journey
To this meaningless, fugitive world.

The priest asks the girl why she returns to the old ruins
of the shrine on the same day each year, and she tells him it
was the day when Genji visited the shrine. He brought with
him a twig of sakaki wood that he pushed through the fence
to tell Rokujō he was there. The priest as he listens enters
into the story and joins in remembrances of the past:

PRIEST: —And the sakaki branch
You hold in your hand
Is the same color it was in the past.

GIRL: The same color as in the past?
Yes, just as you said:
Only the sakaki stays green forever,
And in its unvarying shade,

PRIEST: On the pathways through the wood,
The autumn deepens

GIRL: And leaves turn crimson only to scatter.

PRIEST: In the weed-grown fields

CHORUS: The stalks and leaf tips wither;
Nonomiya, the Shrine in the Fields,
Stands amidst the desolation
Of withered stalks and leaves.
The seventh day of the ninth month
Has returned again today
To this place of memories.

The last passage is sung by the chorus, eight or ten men
seated at stage left. Who are these men? In a Greek tragedy

we would know that they were the Elders of Thebes or the
Women of Troy or the Daughters of Oceanus; but the Nō
chorus has no identity. Often it speaks for the characters in
their voice, occasionally it continues their thoughts or comments on them, but it never speaks in its own voice. A play
like *Nonomiya* may seem more like a dramatic poem than
drama itself, but that is not the experience of anyone who
has seen it performed. Toward the end of the play, Lady
Rokujō, who has revealed herself in her true appearance,
addresses the priest, though first the chorus speaks for her:

CHORUS: I realize now
               That all that happened
               Was surely retribution
               For sins of former lives.
               Even now I am in agony:
               Like the wheels of my carriage
               I return again and again—
               How long must I still keep returning?
               I beg you, dispel this delusion!
               I beg you, dispel my suffering!
ROKUJO: Remembering the vanished days
               I dance, waving at the moon
               My flowerlike sleeves,
CHORUS: As if begging it to restore the past.
ROKUJO: Even the moon
               At the Shrine in the Fields
               Must remember the past;
CHORUS: Its light forlornly trickles
               Through the leaves to the forest dew,
               Through the leaves to the forest dew.
ROKUJO: This place, once my refuge,
               This garden, still lingers

CHORUS: Unchanged from long ago,
ROKUJO: A beauty nowhere else,
CHORUS: Though transient, insubstantial
ROKUJO: As this little wooden fence
CHORUS: From which he once brushed the dew.
            I, whom he visited,
            And he, my lover too,
            The whole world turned to dreams,
            To aging ruins;
            Whom shall I pine for now?
            The voices of pine-crickets
            Trill *rin, rin,*
            The wind howls:
            How I remember
            Nights at the Shrine in the Fields.

At the very end she goes before the torii gate, the only prop, and starts to walk through, only to hesitate, as if afraid to leave this shrine of so many memories. She passes through, but then returns, and the chorus sings the final words of the play:

        As I pass to and fro through this torii
        I seem to wander on the path of delu-
            sion:
        I waver between life and death.
        The gods will surely reject me!
        Again she climbs in her carriage and
            rides out
        The gate of the Burning House,
        The gate of the Burning House.[1]

1. *Nonomiya,* translated by H. Paul Varley, in Donald Keene, ed., *Twenty Plays of the Nō Theatre* (New York: Columbia University Press, 1970), pp. 184, 185–186, 190–191.

At the end of a performance of *Nonomiya*, or of any of the other great plays, the audience should feel moved in a way that is unique to Nō. It is hard to express the nature of this feeling, but it is surely a combination of the emotions aroused by great poetry, music, dance, and a story of universal and timeless intelligibility.

Not everyone enjoys Nō. Many in the audience doze, somehow able to awaken at key moments. In the past, when commoners were only rarely permitted to attend performances of Nō, they eagerly bought tickets only to discover that they could not understand what was going on. On one such occasion a man tried to leave, but he was informed this would be interpreted as a sign of disrespect to the nobles attending; if he absolutely *had* to leave, he would have to pay an exit fee! The first Europeans who saw Nō were most unappreciative. W. G. Aston, who in 1899 wrote what was for many years the only history of Japanese literature in English, stated, "The Nō are not classical poems. They are too deficient in lucidity, method, coherence, and good taste to deserve this description. . . . As dramas the Nō have little value. There is no action to speak of, and dramatic propriety and effects are hardly thought of." The British diplomat Lord Redesdale, who served in Japan from 1866 to 1870, pronounced the Nō to be "wholly unintelligible."

But perhaps these critics were not, in fact, the first Europeans to attend Nō. Letters from Catholic missionaries written in the 1560s describe Japanese plays treating Biblical subjects—Adam and Eve, Noah's Ark, the Judgment of Solomon, the Birth of Christ, the Last Judgment, etc.— apparently in the form of Nō, with roles assigned to the shite, waki, chorus, and so forth. None of these plays has survived, but one missionary's letter reported their success in winning converts. He declared that the quickest way to the hearts of the Japanese was through the theater.

Another unconventional kind of Nō play was the series written beginning in 1594 commemorating the glory of the tyrant Toyotomi Hideyoshi. One play described his recent visit to see the cherry blossoms at Yoshino; another was devoted to a victorious campaign; still another to his mother, who appeared in the second part of the play as a bodhisattva. Zeami's plays were invariably set in the past of a century or more before, possibly to avoid contamination from excessive worldliness, but these new Nō plays treated events of the previous year. Once the traditional materials and treatment had been enriched by foreign and contemporary stories, one might have expected a new kind of Nō to develop. This did not happen, however, because after the establishment in 1603 of the Tokugawa shogunate, a far more conservative and inflexible government than Hideyoshi's, Nō became frozen into a ritual entertainment without any possibility of new development. Despite efforts to introduce new plays from time to time since then, the repertory of Nō today is essentially the same as in the sixteenth century.

In 1603, the same year as the foundation of the Tokugawa shogunate, Kabuki was first performed in Kyoto. Okuni, reputedly a priestess from the important Shintō shrine at Izumo, led a troupe of dancers who performed little skits, including one in which a regular customer of a brothel banters with the proprietress concerning the ladies of the establishment. The subject matter of this skit reveals how utterly unlike the austere Nō this new form of entertainment was. Instead of looking back to the past, typified by the Heian courtiers and the great warriors of the middle ages, Kabuki insisted on the present. Even when a play was ostensibly set in the past, the sentiments expressed were definitely of the present time; anachronisms were cheerfully tolerated, even positively welcomed, as a thumbing of the nose at tradition. In the Nō theater any suggestion of physical attraction onstage was forbidden, even when (as in the case of the martial hero Yoshitsune and the courtesan Shizuka) the play presented the figures as lovers; decorum was preserved by assigning the role of one of the lovers to a small child, who would not arouse amorous associations. In Kabuki, on the other hand, the performances were at first in the nature of dancing and singing commercials, and the products on sale were the actresses themselves, available after the performance for a fee. Quarrels among customers over just who would have the pleasure of escorting Miss So-and-so from the stage door broke out from time to time.

The government generally looked tolerantly on Kabuki, as it did on the licensed quarters of prostitution, as one way of dissipating the energies and financial resources of the samurai class, who had little to do in an age of peace, but it could not allow disorder. The Kabuki theaters were closed in 1629, and when they reopened, women were not allowed to appear on the stage. Young actors took their place in the female roles, but in 1642 quarrels among samurai for *their* favors resulted in a prohibition of young men. The beneficial result of this government concern over the maintenance of public order was that from 1653 on, all parts in Kabuki were taken by grown men with heads shaven to diminish their physical charms, and Kabuki was forced to become a true form of drama in order to attract audiences. The *onnagata*, or actor who takes the roles of women, contributed more than any other factor to the characteristic combination of real and unreal that is at the heart of Kabuki.

The puppet theatre, known today as Bunraku, came into prominence at almost the same time as Okuni's Kabuki dances. The puppets themselves may be traced back to those used during festivals at temples and shrines during the eleventh century. The name by which they were formerly known, *kugutsu*, has been traced to the Greek word *koukla*, strongly suggesting that the art of puppetry made its way to Japan across the breadth of Asia. The instrument used to accompany Bunraku, the samisen, had come from South China by way of Okinawa in the sixteenth century; its sharp, penetrating sound made it a suitable accompaniment for the dramatic recitations of chanters. The texts of the Bunraku plays were from the first more distinguished than those of Kabuki, if only because the puppets lacked the physical charms of beautiful young women or men that would draw customers to performances. But both theaters were popular with the general public and were in fact rivals for two centuries. Until about 1683, when Chikamatsu Monzaemon, usually ranked as the greatest of Japanese dramatists, began to write for the puppets, Kabuki was stronger; but for almost a century thereafter, the puppet theater flourished so conspicuously that one eighteenth-century critic declared that the Kabuki actors might just as well not exist. Eventually the two types of theater developed similar repertories, with the Kabuki actors performing many plays that were originally written for puppets, and yet they remained basically dissimilar; Kabuki is above all a theater of virtuoso actors, while Bunraku is a declaimed and acted literary form.

Kabuki was from the start more realistic than Bunraku, but even so, its plots and stage techniques were highly artificial, and the appearance of male actors in the female roles inevitably produced an effect quite remote from realism. The presence of the onnagata, at first a handicap, came in time to be central to the enjoyment of Kabuki. Audiences continue to this day to admire men, even those who are sixty or seventy years old, in the parts of young women, and one still hears people talk of onnagata who are ravishingly beautiful, though photographs usually do not confirm such views. An onnagata's stage presence alone can create an impression of feminine beauty, and it is really no exaggeration to say that a skillful imitator of women can come closer to the feminine ideal than a real woman. Yoshizawa Ayame (1653–1729), a celebrated onnagata, once said, "If an actress were to appear on the stage she could not express ideal feminine beauty, for she would rely entirely on exploiting her physical charm, and therefore not express the synthetic ideal." Ayame was right: when a great onnagata performs, he displays an almost eerie awareness of his every gesture; nothing is left to chance.

One might suppose that persons who train onnagata would choose feminine-looking young men and give them instruction in falsetto voice production and other elements necessary to convincing portrayals of women. Female impersonators in the West and the actors of female parts in the Chinese opera can persuade audiences that they are looking at real women. But as anyone who has seen a Kabuki performance knows, the great onnagata are not likely to be mistaken for real women. The two finest onnagata of today are ugly when they appear as women, and their voices bring to mind not languishing princesses but the raucous cries of peacocks. Only an inferior onnagata attempts to persuade the audience that he is actually a woman. The ideal of the onnagata being an abstraction of womanhood, the superior onnagata imitates the onnagata of the past, rather than real women.

The dramatist Chikamatsu himself gave the most famous definition of realism in the Japanese theater:

Someone once told me, 'Audiences nowadays will not accept plays unless they are realistic and logical. The old plots are full of nonsense that nobody will tolerate any more. The reputation of Kabuki actors depends on just how realistic their acting seems.' I answered, 'What you say seems plausible, but it does not take into account the true methods of art. Art is something that lies in between reality and unreality. Of course it seems desirable, in view of the current taste for realism, for the actor playing a retainer to copy the gestures and speech of a real retainer, but would a real retainer rouge and powder his face the way actors do? Or, would the audiences like it if an actor, on the grounds that real retainers pay no attention to how they look, were to perform unshaven or displaying a bald head? The theatre is unreal, and yet not unreal, real and yet not real. Entertainment lies between the two.'[2]

With Chikamatsu the popular theater acquired for the first time a master, after decades of hacks who had turned out vehicles for the Kabuki actors, or frustrated Nō actors who had made adaptations of the Nō plays for the puppet stage. Chikamatsu also wrote for the Kabuki actors, but his major works were intended for performance by puppets. He is perhaps the only dramatist of world stature who preferred puppets to actors. It has been suggested that it was because he valued his texts that he made this choice: the Kabuki actors have always felt free to modify texts to enhance the appeal of the plays for the audience or merely to enhance their own parts, but this was impossible in the puppet theater, where the need for perfect coordination of narrator, samisen player, and puppet makes unlikely any deviation from the text. Chikamatsu's puppet plays are written in highly poetic language that ennobles the rather sordid love suicides of shop clerks and prostitutes; his Kabuki texts, by contrast, lead up to the great display pieces for the actor—a

2. My translation, in Donald Keene, ed., *Anthology of Japanese Literature* (New York: Grove Press, 1955), p. 389.

mad scene, for example—and then leave a blank for the actor to fill with his own dialogue.

To this day, Kabuki is a theater of actors. One goes to see Utaemon or Tamasaburō or Shōroku perform, and the play is of secondary interest. Though every last foot soldier or maidservant in the cast is identified, the program generally does not mention the author of the play because it is tacitly accepted that whatever the original dramatist may have written, the text has been much altered over the decades. When the Kabuki actor strikes a notable pose or declaims a speech with special vigor or dances with particular elegance, people in the audience will shout his name or some variant on it. If a protégé of an actor is making his debut, no one will take it amiss if the actor steps out of character and asks the audience to extend its favor to the protégé. One is never allowed to forget the actor, though it is expected that one will forget the author, and the plays are seldom even identified by their original titles. The Nō actors, even when they perform roles that do not require masks, manage to drain from their faces any suggestion of their individuality; in order to *become* the people they portray, they invariably gaze into the mirror before they appear on stage. Nobody ever calls their names during or after a performance. The Bunraku performers are almost as selfless: before the play begins, the chanter, in respect, always lifts to his head the text he is about to recite; even if he knows every syllable by heart, he turns the pages at the appropriate times, so as not to seem to have "mastered" the text. A chanter who is totally blind does the same. The contrast with the self-centered Kabuki actors could not be greater.

I hope that I have suggested the variety of the traditional Japanese theater, one of the wonders of the world. Again and again it has been predicted that one or another kind of theater is destined to perish as soon as a certain actor, a certain maker of Nō masks, a certain carver of heads for the puppet theater dies. Prophets of gloom always manage to sound convincing, but fortunately, they are as likely to be mistaken as any other kind of fortune-teller. The theater, every variety of it, flourishes today in Japan, and we are all its beneficiaries.

■ GENERAL

Keene, Donald. *World Within Walls: Japanese Literature of the Pre-Modern Era, 1600–1867.* New York: Holt, 1976.

Keene, Donald, ed. *Anthology of Japanese Literature.* New York: Grove Press, 1955.

Konishi Jin'ichi. *A History of Japanese Literature,* 4 vols. Princeton, N. J.: Princeton University Press, 1984–.

Miner, Earl, Hiroko Odagiri, and Robert Morrell. *The Princeton Companion to Japanese Classical Literature.* Princeton, N. J.: Princeton University Press, 1986.

■ AESTHETICS

Keene, Donald. *Landscapes and Portraits: Appreciations of Japanese Culture.* Tokyo: Kodansha International, 1971.

Keene, Donald, trans. *Essays in Idleness: The Tsurezuregusa of Kenkō.* New York: Columbia University Press, 1967.

LaFleur, William R. *The Karma of Words: Buddhism and the Literary Arts in Medieval Japan.* Berkeley: University of California Press, 1983.

Matsui, Sakako. *Natsume Sōseki as a Critic of English Literature*. Tokyo: Centre for East Asian Cultural Studies, 1975.

Tsunoda, Ryusaku, Wm. Theodore de Bary, and Donald Keene. *Sources of Japanese Tradition*. New York: Columbia University Press, 1958.

Ueda, Makoto. *Literary and Art Theories in Japan*. Cleveland: Case-Western Reserve University Press, 1967.

■ POETRY

Brower, Robert H. and Earl Miner. *Japanese Court Poetry*. Stanford, Calif.: Stanford University Press, 1961.

Levy, Ian Hideo. *Hitomaro and the Birth of Japanese Lyricism*. Princeton, N. J.: Princeton University Press, 1984.

Levy, Ian Hideo, trans. *Man'yōshū*. 4 vols. Princeton, N. J., Princeton University Press, 1981–.

McCullough, Helen Craig. *Brocade by Night: "Kokin Wakashū" and the Court Style in Japanese Classical Poetry*. Stanford, Calif.: Stanford University Press, 1985.

McCullough, Helen Craig, trans. *Kokin Wakashū: The First Imperial Anthology of Japanese Poetry*. Stanford, Calif.: Stanford University Press, 1985.

The Manyōshū. The Nippon Gakujutsu Shinkōkai translation. New York: Columbia University Press, 1965.

Miner, Earl. *Japanese Linked Poetry*. Princeton, N. J.: Princeton University Press, 1979.

Philippi, Donald L., trans. *Kojiki*. Tokyo: University of Tokyo Press, 1968.

Rodd, Laurel Rasplica, trans., with Mary Catherine Henkenius. *Kokinshū*. Princeton, N. J.: Princeton University Press, 1984.

Sato, Hiroaki and Burton Watson, trans. *From the Country of Eight Islands: An Anthology of Japanese Poetry*. Garden City, N. Y.: Doubleday, 1981; New York: Columbia University Press, Morningside Books, 1986.

■ FICTION

De Bary, Wm. Theodore, trans. *Five Women Who Loved Love* (Ihara Saikaku). Rutland, Vt.: Tuttle, 1956.

Field, Norma. *The Splendor of Longing in "The Tale of Genji."* Princeton, N. J.: Princeton University Press, 1987.

Hibbett, Howard. *The Floating World in Japanese Fiction.* New York: Oxford University Press, 1959.

Kitagawa, Hiroshi and Bruce T. Tsuchida, trans. *The Tale of the Heike.* Tokyo: Tokyo University Press, 1975.

McCullough, Helen Craig. *Tales of Ise: Lyrical Episodes from Tenth-Century Japan.* Stanford, Calif.: Stanford University Press, 1968.

Morris, Ivan, trans. *The Life of an Amorous Woman* (Ihara Saikaku). New York: New Directions, 1963.

Nosco, Peter, trans. *Some Final Words of Advice* (Ihara Saikaku). Tokyo: Tuttle, 1980.

Rimer, J. Thomas. *Modern Japanese Fiction and Its Traditions.* Princeton, N. J.: Princeton University Press, 1978. (Includes a translation of *Taketori Monogatari.*)

Sargent, G. W., trans. *The Japanese Family Storehouse.* Cambridge: Cambridge University Press, 1959.

Seidensticker, Edward G., trans. *The Tale of Genji* (Murasaki Shikibu). 2 vols. New York: Knopf, 1976.

Shirane, Haruo. *The Bridge of Dreams: A Poetics of "The Tale of Genji."* Stanford, Calif.: Stanford University Press, 1987.

Waley, Arthur, trans. *The Tale of Genji* (Murasaki Shikibu). New York: Random House, Modern Library, 1960.

Zolbrod, Leon M., trans. *Ugetsu Monogatari* (by Ueda Akinari). London: Allen and Unwin, 1974.

■ THEATER

Adachi, Barbara C. *Backstage at Bunraku.* New York and Tokyo: Weatherhill, 1985.

Brandon, James R. *Chūshingura: Studies in Kabuki and the Puppet Theater.* Honolulu: University of Hawaii Press, 1982.

Gerstle, C. Andrew. *Circles of Fantasy: Convention in the Plays of Chikamatsu.* Cambridge, Mass.: Harvard University Press, 1986.

Gunji, Masakatsu. *Kabuki.* Tokyo: Kodansha International, 1985.

Keene, Donald. *Bunraku.* Tokyo: Kodansha International, 1965.

Keene, Donald. *Nō, the Classical Theatre of Japan.* Tokyo: Kodansha International, 1966.

Keene, Donald, trans. *Chūshingura.* New York: Columbia University Press, 1971.

Keene, Donald, trans. *Major Plays of Chikamatsu.* New York: Columbia University Press, 1961.

Keene, Donald, ed. *Twenty Plays of the Nō Theatre.* New York: Columbia University Press, 1970.